A TIDEWATER MORNING

William Styron is the Pulitzer Prize-winning author of *The Long March*, *Lie Down in Darkness*, *Set This House on Fire*, *The Confessions of Nat Turner* and *Sophie's Choice*. He has also published *Darkness Visible*, the remarkable story of his descent into depression, a collection, *This Quiet Dust and Other Writings*, and *A Tidewater Morning*. He lives in Roxbury, Connecticut, and Martha's Vineyard.

ALSO BY WILLIAM STYRON

The Long March
Lie Down in Darkness
Set This House on Fire
The Confessions of Nat Turner
Sophie's Choice
This Quiet Dust
Darkness Visible

William Styron

A TIDEWATER MORNING

Three Tales from Youth

VINTAGE

Published by Vintage 2001

2 4 6 8 10 9 7 5 3 1

Copyright © William Styron 1993

William Styron has asserted his right under the Copyright, Designs and Patents Act 1988 to be identified as the author of this work

'Love Day' was originally published in *Esquire* magazine in 1985. 'Shadrach' was originally published in *Esquire* in 1978. 'A Tidewater Morning' was originally published in *Esquire* in 1987.

First published in Great Britain in 1993 by
Jonathan Cape

Vintage
Random House, 20 Vauxhall Bridge Road,
London SW1V 2SA

Random House Australia (Pty) Limited
20 Alfred Street, Milsons Point, Sydney
New South Wales 2061, Australia

Random House New Zealand Limited
18 Poland Road, Glenfield, Auckland 10,
New Zealand

Random House (Pty) Limited
Endulini, 5A Jubilee Road, Parktown 2193,
South Africa

The Random House Group Limited Reg. No. 954009
www.randomhouse.co.uk

A CIP catalogue record for this book
is available from the British Library

ISBN 0 09 928553 3

Papers used by Random House are natural, recyclable products made from wood grown in sustainable forests. The manufacturing processes conform to the environmental regulations of the country of origin

Printed and bound in Great Britain by
Cox & Wyman Limited, Reading, Berkshire

TO CARLOS FUENTES

The long habit of living indisposeth us for dying.

—SIR THOMAS BROWNE, *Urn Burial*

CONTENTS

AUTHOR'S NOTE

These narratives reflect the experiences of the author at the ages of twenty, ten, and thirteen. The tales are an imaginative reshaping of real events and are linked by a chain of memories.

The memories are of a single place—the Virginia Tidewater of the 1930s. This was a region occupied with preparations for war. It was not the drowsy Old Virginia of legend but part of a busy New South, where heavy industry and the presence of the military had begun to encroach on a pastoral way of life.

Ironically, such an intrusion doubtless helped many of the people, white and black, to survive the worst of the Great Depression.

—W. S.

Love Day

On April Fool's Day, 1945 (which was also Easter Sunday), the Second Marine Division, in which Doug Stiles and I were platoon leaders, made an assault on the southeast coast of Okinawa. Actually this was a fake assault, and we had problems about that. Anyway, on the same day, fifteen miles to the north, the First and Sixth Marine divisions, together with two Army divisions, moved ashore in an area of the island coast known as the Hagushi beaches, where the troops met no resistance on a clear, balmy spring morning. Okinawa was the last stepping-stone before the Japanese mainland. It was by far the largest invasion since the landing in Normandy, and the most massive operation of the Pacific war. Although the enemy didn't make an appearance during the first few days, the Japanese and American troops eventually clashed with enormous violence, producing more casualties on both sides than any other campaign in the Pacific. But this took place weeks later.

Stiles and I were both lean, mean, splendidly trained young lieutenants, hungry for Japanese heads. Together we had learned to become infantry officers at Camp Lejeune, at Quantico, in the boondocks around San Diego, and finally on Saipan—the divisional staging area for the assault on Okinawa. We were weapons experts, knew the subtleties of infantry tactics, all the tricks of cover and concealment, night fighting, bayonet fighting, knife fighting, ground-to-air communication—everything. We could with no queasiness whatever handle grenades and high explosives. We possessed beautifully honed killers' skills, waiting to be tried. We were proud of the powers of leadership that would make us able to goad several dozen troops through enemy fire over terrain of every type of wetness and dryness and alien loathsomeness. As physical specimens we were also appallingly fit.

Lolling these later years before the flickering tube, I have viewed golden lads in the surf or snow, twisting and swerving with the grace of antelopes; this may cause me a twitch of nostalgia, but also an admiration totally ungrudging, since I can truthfully say, "Paul Whitehurst was once like that." Never again in my life would my health have such incandescence as it did at twenty. The ambition of my years of puberty—when I was literally and disgracefully a ninety-eight-pound weakling—was finally achieved: I had real muscles, and I knew how to use them. I smoked cigarettes, but so did nearly all Marines, and this seemed to have no effect on my senses, which responded as delicately to the ambient air as those of an Apache scout. Over all this manly pulchritude was spread a patina of golden suntan. I was the ideal size for a Marine platoon leader, which is to say tall but not excessively so, well fleshed but not brawny: guys that were too big made a fine target for a Jap bullet.

Stiles had always been a natural athlete—among other things, a champion swimmer at Yale—and therefore had had no need to gloat, as I did, over the supple strength we had gained from unending hours of pooping and snooping. Another thing that united us (and I can look back only with wonder at this part of our conditioned behavior) was our almost complete absence of fear.

Almost, I say. In the privacy of our most searching and intimate conversation Stiles and I both confessed to a healthy amount of the gut-heaving frights and willies that any infantryman feels at the prospect of battle. But a Marine platoon leader is a bit like a scoutmaster who, in taking his tykes on a tramp through the woods, encounters murky, nearly unfordable streams, poisonous rattlesnakes, nests of vicious wasps, huge grizzly bears. Though scared half out of his wits himself by these threats and obstacles, the scoutmaster has to make a stout show of it and display no loss of nerve, lest the little troop get infected by the fright oozing out of him and then scatter everywhere, irretrievably disbanded.

A Marine platoon leader—in those days rating highest in death risk among all U.S. service ranks and categories—must therefore, paradoxically, appear the bravest while having the greatest cause for terror. Scores of second lieutenants had, only weeks before, been butchered like calves on Iwo Jima. Stiles and I discussed this frequently, with a certain wryness of tone. Yet while admitting freely to passing spasms of sickening fear, we both concluded that our need to constantly *display* coolness and imperturbability made us, to a large extent, cool and imperturbable, until fear itself began to settle far aft amid the cargo of other mixed concerns and emotions. In the first place, we were on the go nearly every day and too busy to pay much attention to fear. Furthermore, we welcomed the prospect of battle, yearned for its perils and its challenges and excitement. After all, it was not to obtain some sedentary administrative sinecure that we joined the Corps. For that we could have joined the Army. We joined for the glamour, the toughness, for the sense of belonging to the most gallant of warrior orders. And out of some nearly inscrutable passion—mingling the desire to kill with the thrill of risking death—we embraced the giddiest ideal of virility. "God Bless America" and the fight against evil had a great deal to do with it, of course—we all thought it a noble war— but the patriotic motif was secondary. I think we might have loved the Marines had the Corps been Finnish or Greek. Basically, I believe we wanted to become modestly proportioned but alluring icons of our era; by shooting a squad or two of maniacal Japs, we would cover ourselves with glory and Silver Stars, come back to the States on leave to screw a flock of eager girls, and with our tailored forest-green uniforms and sparkling gold bars stride down the street looking every bit as heroic as Tyrone Power. We would have been embarrassed to concern ourselves much about fear.

You can imagine our chagrin, then, when just after we sailed from Saipan we learned that the division's assault on Okinawa—a five-day voyage away—was no assault at all but a feint, a diversion. There would be no landing of the troops. Instead, while the other Marine and Army units were staging their real invasion to the north, we would be engaged in a mock amphibious attack: scores of landing craft churning toward the coast under protective clouds of smoke, halting at the last moment, wheeling about, then returning to the fleet of mother ships standing offshore—the entire demonstration, of course, intended to deceive the Japanese forces and suck them away from the authentic invaders storming the Hagushi beaches. After this hollow and pretentious display, the division would be placed in a status known as floating reserve. That meant day after day of wallowing about on intolerably confining ships, enduring stupefying tedium, eating food that became increasingly vile owing to long storage, and waiting for the moment to arrive when everyone would be put ashore to finally get a taste of battle. So far, so good—action-starved Marines could put up with nearly anything so long as they got a shot at the enemy sooner or later—but there was an ominous hitch. Rumors had been spreading before L (for Love) Day morning that after the fake assault and the interminable hours afloat we

7

would not be called upon to fight at all, but instead would steam back to our enchanted Saipan, with its empty nights and its Abbott and Costello movies. To Stiles and me, this was a monumental swindle. Also, the mood of our troops, as they sweated and stirred about belowdecks of the USS *General Washburn,* was bewildered, restless, and depressed. They were gung ho, too, and itching to fight, and while there may have been a few boys relieved to be let off the hook, so to speak, I think most of them were left sullenly disappointed by this turn of events. The only danger we would be exposed to was real but somehow vulgar, freakish, base: kamikaze attacks. To be on a ship that was a victim of a kamikaze plane would be as ignominious as getting run over by a laundry truck.

A troopship may be the most disagreeable domestic environment devised by man—a cramped, fetid space occupied by quintuple the number of human beings it was designed to accommodate. Men slept in bunks or hammocks so tightly squeezed together that the reclining bodies looked like slabs of meat packed for the market wagons. No prison on earth could rival the bowels of a troopship for incessant noise: the stridor and bellowing of hundreds of voices, feet thumping, snoring, cackles, whistles, weapons clanging against deck and bulkhead, and over all the groaning and grinding of the ship itself as it rocked its way through vast seas. Troops could not walk in these jammed and suffocating quarters; they sidled sideways, rump to groin, in an atmosphere that smelled of bodies, bad breath, cooking, flatulence, and quite often vomit, for seasickness was endemic and by no means confined to lads from the Great Plains. The dumb-ox queues that are a common feature of military life took on here, throughout the dim passageways of a troopship, a kind of squalid end-lessness—three-hour-long lines for food, two-hour lines for the shower, squirming lines for the toilets, even lines to allow the troops in regulated shifts to emerge from their tomb and breathe for a brief spell the salty air of the foredeck or fantail.

In good weather the deck was a refuge, and it was here, in the afternoon—perhaps eighteen hours before our "assault" on Okinawa—that I fell asleep, shielded from the wind by a hatchway cover while I dreamed the most troubled, confusing, and unbearably sad dreams I could ever try to remember. They had to do with my childhood and with my mother and father, but were resonant with no echo of serenity, no mood of repose, containing rather a vague but fearful augury of the never-endingness of war. I woke up suddenly, not in my usual spirit of businesslike enthusiasm, but over-whelmed by sorrow and with longing for something quite unnameable. Feeling the great ship shimmying beneath me, I blinked out at the swelling ocean billows and realized I had suffered almost my first real attack of homesickness since I had been in the Pacific. But what was the message of those dreams? I wondered. Why had they made me feel so vulnerable, so helpless—so little like a Marine, so much like a lost boy?

Stiles was gazing down at me when I awoke. He had an expression of sullen gloom, and the unhappiness suffused his face, which was one of those homely-handsome Anglo-Saxon faces with a slightly hooked, prominent patrician nose, shrewd hazel eyes, and big, square, flashing teeth that dominated his looks gleefully when he laughed—and he was a great laugher. But today he was gray with glumness. He was wearing a regulation sweatshirt and shorts, and held in his hand a Modern Library edition of Hobbes's *Leviathan*. He reached down and gave me a tug upward until I stood erect and then walked with him toward the rail, the two of us threading our way through several dozen Marines sprawled out on the deck, cleaning the M-1s and BARs for the tenth or twentieth or thirtieth time on the voyage.

"You've heard the scuttlebutt, haven't you?" he said, as we leaned on the rail. Approaching Okinawa, the *General Washburn* had slowed to what seemed about three-quarters speed, and the rest of the fleet had slowed, too. We gazed at the immense armada steaming northward on all sides of us—scores of troop transports and supply ships, at least one flattop of the *Essex* class, a couple of battlewagons, and, far out on the flanks, a pack of darting destroyer-escorts, moving like swift, nervous sheepdogs as they rode herd on our lumbering way through a breezy sea flecked with foam and spin-drift. "The scuttlebutt," Stiles went on, "is that we won't be landing on Okinawa, even after we're put in floating reserve. Someone said that Happy Halloran thinks the whole division's going to be sent back to Saipan."

"Well," I said, "what do you know about that?" My tone was blasé, but the distress, the instant sense of letdown, was like the grip of nausea in my stomach. "How can you be so sure?" I paused. "Shit!"

"I don't know," Stiles replied, "but the Old Man's almost always right about things like that." He paused and looked skyward. "You seen any action today?"

He was speaking of battles in the air. As the fleet had neared Japanese waters, commencing the day before, kamikazes and other Jap planes—fighters and bomb-ers—had been emboldened to strike like hornets during their forays from bases on Kyushu. Yesterday, Stiles and I and hundreds of other cheering Marines had wit-nessed from the ship's deck a dogfight such as most of us had seen only in the Fox Movietone newsreels. It had been so close overhead that I did not need my binocu-lars: a Zero and a Hellcat in a marvelous spiraling duel, the American at first dominating the skirmish, the shiny bullet of a plane swooping in pursuit of its prey unshakably and with such precision that the move-ments of the two enemies seemed to possess, for an instant, an almost loverlike choreography; then, in a swift twist impossible to follow, the Jap close behind the

Hellcat, spurting machine-gun bursts of smoke and pin-pricks of flame; another reversal, the whining screech of both engines very clear now, because lower, almost over the ship's stacks. Then—Jesus!—a sudden explosion, a pluming bituminous beard of smoke, every heart skipping a beat (our boy? theirs?), and now—oh, happiness—the fuselage with its red Rising Sun wobbling seaward like a maimed hawk and plunging into the waves only yards away with the sweet finality those newsreels had shown us ever since Pearl Harbor. "That Jap son of a bitch could fly," Stiles had said appreciatively through the chorus of cheers, as the Hellcat streaked back toward its flattop and we watched a geyser of steam rise from the Zero's tomb, an umbrella of windswept dew receding swiftly southward.

But today, nothing. It was just as well. We needed nothing to distract us from our disappointment.

"We could go see the Old Man," I suggested. "Maybe he'll give it to us straight." I was still afflicted by the somber residue of my dreams, but I was unable to touch the source of my discontent, as if I had been plunged in mourning, but restless mourning for someone whose identity I could not place, someplace once loved but irreparably destroyed.

Lieutenant Colonel Timothy ("Happy") Halloran had a tiny cabin, but it *was* a cabin—as befitted an officer of his rank—and when we entered he was shaving over a washbasin. He scraped around and beneath a truly spellbinding black handlebar mustache. His reflected eyes peered back at us from a small steel mirror that hung from the bulkhead. All the rest I could see was a rear view of his beautifully muscled torso; the shiny scar of a bullet wound near the armpit (this received at Tarawa) enhanced the glamorous presence of a man for whom—during those days—the word "admiration" would sound paltry and stale. Two young priests approaching a monsignor of especial renown and charisma, rookies deferentially making their presence known to Joe DiMaggio, a couple of extremely fresh congressmen seeking counsel from the Speaker of the House—this was the way Stiles and I came to visit Happy Halloran. Our very reverence compelled a certain irreverence, and Halloran himself encouraged informality; he was one of those estimable Marine officers who, without losing a shred of authority, exercised the common touch.

He scratched at his face, ignoring the hoodlum flies—stowaways from Saipan—that buzzed around him. His shaving cream was scented with lavender, which seemed as incongruous as the mere fact of his shaving at this hour—until it occurred to me how very *Halloran* it was. He wanted to make the landing, aborted as it might be, with a reasonably unstubbled face and could be too busy all the rest of the day and night to complete his toilet. I suspect that he also liked to keep his handlebar graphically emphasized. I admired this touch of panache, and I recalled that he had ordered the rest of the battalion to shave themselves, too, whether they needed it or not—and some were young enough not to need to. With Halloran this was not chickenshit but class, and the kids ate it up. I felt passionately that Stiles and I would not have been half the platoon leaders we were had it not been for the example of Halloran. It was total infatuation.

"Hiya, Dougie," he said to Stiles, then to me: "Hiya, Paul, how's your hammer hangin'? Sit down and take a load off."

"Thank you, sir," we said in unison, easing ourselves down on his bunk.

"So the long-awaited confrontation with our reptile foe, me laddies, is going to be but a wee scuffle, without a shot fired in anger." He continued to shave while he uttered these words, which were intended to sound Scottish, I supposed, but resembled no dialect or accent I had ever heard. To me it was a small wart, but such an attempt at mimicry marked the height of his sense of the comic. Even now, through the lather, he was grinning at what he had just said. He had a touch of swarthiness—I supposed he could be described as black Irish—and the dimpled smile that plumped up his cheeks, and his hearty midwestern voice, gave a distant impression of Clark Gable. With whimsical affection I once thought that if you could distill the sheer masculinity he exuded, make of it some volatile essence, you would have an adman's triumph—a cologne called Cock and Balls, smelling of leather, sweat, and gunpowder. At that time he was for me the matchless Marine officer. He was a graduate of the Citadel, where he had focused on engineering and had been made to read Longfellow. He had never heard of Franz Joseph Haydn, Anton Chekhov, or William Blake. But because I was one of his votaries, this ignorance was a virtually uncorrectable defect that made no difference.

Dropping the brogue, he glanced by way of the mirror at Stiles's book and said: "What learned pundit are you sticking your nose into now, Dougie?"

"Hobbes, sir," Stiles replied, "an English philosopher of the seventeenth century. The book's called *Leviathan.* It's probably his chef d'oeuvre."

In the mirror I could see Halloran grinning. "Give me an abstract. Is he Bolshie or anti-Bolshie?"

After a hesitation, Stiles said: "Well, it's hard to be specific, sir, since his historical context was so complicated, and he predated Marx by so many years. I suppose you could say that in his concept of the State as a kind of supermonster he was providing us, willy-nilly, with one of the earliest critiques of the Communist form of totalitarianism. But then at the same time you could hardly call him an advocate of democracy."

"He'd be to the right of that other guy, then—what's his name, John Locke?"

"Oh, certainly," Stiles said. "By comparison Locke would be a true liberal."

Halloran ruminated for a moment, holding his straight-edge razor poised in midair. "How much influence did this guy have on Marx? As much as Hegel?"

"Oh, God, no," Stiles said, "no one influenced Marx so much as Hegel. Oh, I'm sure Marx had read the great English social philosophers—Hobbes, Locke, Bentham—but he pretty much discarded their ideas and created his own system."

"That Marx," said Halloran, shaking his head, "that fucking Marx. What a shitload of trouble."

He paused and flipped a blob of foam from his razor, the straight-edge blade murderous-looking and slender, the only nonsafety razor in the outfit, to my knowledge, and nearly the only one I had ever seen. It was among the colonel's trademarks, like the handlebar mustache or the silver-inlaid Colt .38 special police revolver he wore on his hip in a luxurious cordovan leather holster so energetically spit-shined that once, collapsed down beside him during a training problem on a Saipan beach, I saw my face bulbously reflected in it, as in a fun-house mirror. Both the Jerry Colonna mustache and the revolver were nonregulation; mustaches were allowed but they should not be recherché, and the standard-issue sidearm was a .45 automatic. The automatic, it was commonly noted, was not really reliable, hard to aim (though once aimed it could pulverize an ox). But it was less for this reason that Halloran sported his more glamorous sidearm—and the flamboyant handlebar—than for their dash and style, to which his status as a legend entitled him. The Marine Corps is rigorous, even Prussian, in many of its fetishlike requirements, but there is something affectingly lackadaisical in its tolerance of reasonable eccentricities shown by favored odd-balls; unlike the Prussians, the Marines, thanks to this good-natured view, have been helped in saving themselves from dementia.

"So you think this Hobbes can help you devastate Marx when you get down to that book you're planning to write?" Halloran asked.

"Yes, sir, absolutely," Stiles said. "A man whose evil has been so vast and pervasive has had to draw his ideas from many sources, and I don't want to miss even a fragment of the thought that might have been provided by any of his predecessors."

"Well, as I say, I keep wishing you luck." He paused again. "That fucking Marx sure brought us a shitload of trouble."

I rather hoped this part of the conversation would cease, since I'd heard it or its equivalent several times before. In the Marines, political talk among officers has traditionally been constrained by a lurking delicacy that makes it almost forbidden (it *is* forbidden in officers' wardrooms, along with religion and sex); but the Bolshevik menace, I had discovered, could be fair game. Like most regular officers Halloran was a political dumbbell, and Stiles had become his mentor. As for myself, I was considerably less interested in politics than Stiles was, and his involvement could become annoyingly overheated. But suddenly and mercifully the matter evaporated. We watched for a moment while Halloran swabbed his cheeks with a towel, then patted on talcum powder. Shortly, I knew from past observation, he would carefully wax the mustache with something he called "twice-precious goo" from a jar he had acquired in San Francisco's Chinatown. But even as he stroked his cheeks, exhaling in satisfaction, we heard over the churning of the ship's engines a far-off booming sound, sensed an ugly vibration in the air; for an instant all three of us cocked our ears. Then we relaxed. It could have been anything, way out on the sea: a kamikaze obliterating a destroyer, a flattop like *Intrepid* or *Essex* being torpedoed, an ammo ship reduced to iron filings and vapor—anything. Halloran, still peering into the mirror, silently mouthed the words "Fuck it."

"Sir," said Stiles, "what's this scuttlebutt about the division going back to Saipan? Is it true that we might not *ever* make a landing?"

"I can't say for sure, Dougie," Halloran replied, "but I wouldn't be surprised. There's all sorts of poop filtering down from G-2 that we won't be needed. Now, please, don't ask me why. But the word's out that in Washington, or Pearl, or wherever such decisions are made, they believe our two divisions plus the dogface divisions will be quite enough. If this is so, it's back to our old island and all that wild nightlife in Garapan."

"But Jesus, sir!" Stiles was on his feet, slamming his fist into his palm, all agitation and protest. "This is a farce! We didn't come out here these thousands of miles to sit around that stinking little island and watch our hands and feet rot off. We were trained to kill Japs, for

Christ's sake! And now there's this phony operation tomorrow just to tease us. That wouldn't be so bad if we knew we were at least being held in reserve, that we'd be landed sooner or later. But *this*! To go back to Saipan and turn into zombies! It's"—his voice rose querulously—"it's intolerable!"

"Calm down, Douglas, me boy," Halloran said amiably, lapsing into an Irish brogue now, excruciating but somewhat more convincing than the Highland cadence; he was, after all, of Irish descent. "In the Corps ye'll learn to endure frustration and take orders like the foine young lad you are. If you don't make Okinawa, you'll surely make the mainland. Then on the mainland, it's me foine belief, ye'll get to kill yourself half a dozen of the little ringtail baboons—maybe half a hundred. Also," he added with a lewd wink, "you'll get a lot of that sidewise nooky." He was alluding to the Marine Corps pleasantry, exhaustively repeated, that the Japanese pudendum was horizontal.

"But the mainland! God knows when that'll be. Anything could happen. We could get sick, have an accident—anything!" Stiles stopped for a moment, resumed in a milder voice: "With all due respect, sir, and no offense, but you've personally taken care of a bunch of those baboons. We haven't." He spread his arm in a gesture that included me, wearing an expression that made him seem embarrassingly close to grief. "We haven't laid eyes on a Jap!"

There was another dullish *crump crump,* closer now,

near enough to make the colonel's eyebrows twitch. "Kamikaze," he said, and stretched out his body toward the porthole. "Fucking Japanese lunatics," he murmured in a flat, emotionless voice, searching the ocean. "Insane sons of bitches. Fucking dogs, whole fucking empire. Eighty million animals with rabies." He drew back from the porthole, licked his lips, inhaled, strove to say something else, then trailed off with a valiant but somehow inadequate "Dog fuckers." Suddenly a sparkle lit in his eyes—it was plain he was finished with Stiles's spunky dissidence—and he said: "Well, let's have a drop of whiskey, me boys, and I'll tell you a little story."

And suddenly I didn't want to hear a story. I was seized once again by the despondent, haunted mood that had overtaken me on the deck. I felt that sharp homesickness again and yearned to return to sleep. But I had to hear (or pretend to hear) the story, even though Halloran was one of the worst storytellers I had ever listened to. Someone (it may have been Stiles) remarked that when Halloran got halfway through a story, even Halloran began to go to sleep. Lest I be misunderstood, this had nothing to do with intelligence but arose from a particular deafness—not just a lack of savoir faire but deafness to all social nuance, like a hymn singer caroling with glorious self-confidence Sunday after Sunday in just noticeably the wrong tempo and a halftone flat. Halloran was such a splendid fighting man that everyone pardoned his buffoonery. Stiles, who revered Halloran as much as I did, but who likewise wondered what made the man tick, once laid it all out to me in what I thought was a deft analysis. Happy Halloran was a *professional Marine*. He was 101 percent Marine Corps—member of a fellowship of knights, professor of a faith, a way of life to which he had consecrated himself as fiercely as any guardian of the Grail. Okay, Stiles went on, this Illinois knight served his squire's discipline at Culver Military Academy. Then the Citadel, where the intellectual level was on a par with that of a night school for the mentally retarded. Then the time served with the Fourth Marines in Shanghai just before Pearl Harbor. The Americans, along with the British and the French, had made a playground of Shanghai for years. Probably the only time as an adult he'd had any taste of a civilian atmosphere—eating wonton soup and trying to make out with all that fabled blond White Russian pussy. Then at last these years of war—virtually the rest of his life (except for a brief Stateside assignment)—spent among the sweltering Pacific isles, fighting an enemy he hated with such barely governed rage that he choked when he uttered its name. Wouldn't you, Stiles said to me, be a little—ahem—*peculiar*, I mean not quite like the rest of us college kids, if that was the earliest chapter in the story of *your* life as an American boy?

The colonel poured a couple of fingers of whiskey into three mess-kit cups and sat down on the edge of the bunk opposite us. It was strictly illegal to drink aboard ship—but, of course, fuck it. Like all Marines who had been in the Pacific for many months, Halloran was scandalously rich through accumulated and unspent back pay. "I gave a Navy supply officer seventy-five bucks for this bottle," he said, grinning, and held the fifth of amber-hued bourbon up to the light. "Old Forester. Only the best for gents of the Second Battalion. I don't think I told you this story before, fellows—"

A beer guzzler, I had tasted whiskey only half a dozen times in my life; I didn't yet quite know how to handle the awesomely poetic exhilaration I felt when it began nibbling away at my brain cells. I took a hefty sip and experienced instant vertigo: this canceled out any need to try to follow Halloran's narrative. The only story I wished I *could* hear—an account from his own lips of the fabulous episode on Tarawa that had won him the Navy Cross (and, of course, our houndlike devotion)— was obviously the only story that he, like any hero with appropriate modesty, could not tell. Instead (oh, Jesus, I thought), here began another tale about Shanghai, the poor guy's golden time of whoopee amid a totally regimented life. Would it be about Svetlana, the honey-haired White Russian "countess," suspected agent for the Japanese, who tried her sultry best to squeeze out secrets from Halloran, the junior intelligence officer? (It was a story with brilliant possibilities, and it should have had zip and suspense, like a good Hitchcock movie, in addition to some juicy sex, but Halloran had told it so confusedly that it lacked all of these, especially the sex. "Svetlana was just a slut" was his raciest observation, which reinforced my view that, like most military academy men, he was basically quite prudish, all talk and small action, and had probably gotten less ass than even I had.) Or would it be about Chinese beer? Halloran could do a minimum of forty-five minutes on the brewing of Chinese beer and still be working up to matters of bottle design and the way the head foamed.

"Shanghai." I heard the word and I shut Halloran off from my mind as if I had snapped a switch. The eyes of many people, when confronted with a bore, glaze over; one can actually see the glaze as it steals over their vision, a gradual lusterlessness that becomes like that of raw oysters long exposed to air. I, by contrast, have always had the knack of being able to maintain pinpoints of light in my pupils, giving the bore a false impression that I am listening. Thus, as Halloran wound himself up in his reminiscence, and my nostalgia deepened, I sank into a reverie while two interlocking memories flickered in my head like scenes from a home movie. The faraway explosions had made me envision an aircraft carrier in its death convulsion; I had a swift image of oily smoke boiling heavenward, the deck listing, sailors tumbling into the sea like scattered windup toys. This dissolved, gave way to the memory of the launching of the flattop *Ranger*, America's first aircraft carrier, which, at the age of seven, I believed to be largely the creation of my father—although he was

actually only a medium-level draftsman at the shipyard, where he took me (drugged with sleep at three in
the morning) to gawk and marvel.

   And it *had* been thrilling to watch the mechanics, at
once brutish and delicate, of setting loose the behemoth
into its natural element—of freeing from its uterine dry
dock into the strife-torn seas the "biggest, most complex
and costly movable object made by human hands" (my
father's words). It had required nine hours, this monstrous parturition, set into motion long before dawn by
gangs of floodlit chanting Negroes swinging oak batter-
ing rams that knocked down, at precisely timed inter-
vals, one after another of the scores of telephone
pole—sized pilings that for months had held in equipoise
thousands of tons of inert steel. "A marvel of technology!" said my father. I was enraptured by this sight: the
sweating black figures sang in a rhythmic chorus, wild,
scary, African. It was controlled bedlam, and it was also
splendidly dangerous. Now and then a pole would split
apart nastily, or topple the wrong way, and the Negroes
would drop the ram with a thunderous noise and scatter
for their lives (unprotected to any degree, I might add,
by collective bargaining). Their labor ended at the
stroke of noon, when two events took place almost
together. First, in an act of godlike finality, Mr.
Gresham, an engineer colleague of my father's,
hunched down deep in a pit beneath the hull, pressed
a button that detonated a dynamite cap, blowing off the
top of the single upright that remained. "Imagine such

---

a delicate balance!" my father whispered, or rather shouted above the crowd's roar as the mass of gray steel, bunting-bedecked, began to slip ever so gently toward the muddy James. What a sight—this new sweetheart of the seas being birthed, lubricated in its passage down the ways by dirty white masses of tallow as high as snowdrifts. The tallow slithered out from beneath the keel in gigantic curlicues and sent afloat to the festive onlookers a smell of rancid mutton. At nearly the same instant that Mr. Gresham pushed his button, I heard Mrs. Herbert Hoover warble: "I christen thee *Ranger*!" I noticed that her slip was showing, and then she went *clunk* with the bottle, *clunk* again at the prow sliding away from her before she solidly connected, showering the *Ranger* and herself with a purple sacrament of Prohibition grape juice. A week or two later, in one of the newsreels, I actually caught a blurred half-second glimpse of myself, gaping up at my father adoringly.

But there is something else you forgot, I thought, as I sat in Halloran's cabin and felt the bourbon warming me, making my lips grow numb. You forgot your father's voice on the ride homeward: *"Someday planes will fly off that ship and bomb the Japanese."* You believed your father as you believed—then—in God, but did not believe this, believed only that it was a joke he was making about war. War was in the movies, war was not something that ever happened, not to Americans . . .

"I had this pal in Shanghai then," I heard Halloran say. "A Marine gunner named Willie Weldon. He was a little older than I was, an old China hand who'd been with Rupertus's battalion back in the mid-1930s, when the Japs were kicking up their usual shit." I suddenly realized that I had let my Halloran switch go to the On position, and I nodded and smiled again, half-listening. "Well. Willie Weldon was one of the biggest swordsmen that ever came down the pike. The rank of gunner really fit him. This guy was absolutely crazy for gash. Anyway, I told Willie I'd introduce him to this friend of Svetlana's. A gal named Ludmilla, a really good-looking stacked White Russian broad who lived in a great flat right off Bubbling Well Road." He paused and scratched his chin. "No, it was near the Nanking Road, I remember, because Bubbling Well had been blocked off to traffic——"

You're losing me, Colonel, I thought, ready to drift away again. *Un raconteur de longues histoires,* I wanted to tell him, must be direct, linear, must not encumber his tales with the distracting names of thoroughfares, above all must be deft and relevant, *relevant:* For God's sake, keep the ball moving! "I think her name was Ludmilla, or maybe it was the other one, Olga. Fuck! I can't remember. No, wait a minute——"

Whenever, I thought—switching Halloran off again—whenever I was overtaken by a spasm of metaphysical creepiness, and the sheer unreality of this endless war enfolded me like a damp, mildewed shroud, I thought of my father. How could he have been so prescient? How could he have known those many years ago that I would someday be in a situation like this? How did he ever imagine that his son would grow up to be a killer, not only willing but eager to kill—to anticipate killing with crude, erotic excitement? He didn't know the last part. But of course it now seemed inevitable that he—a man who helped build huge war machines but who was a peaceable soul with an exquisite sense of history—should have visualized the trajectory of his son's life, ending here in these remote and unknown archipelagoes before he was old enough to vote. And I recalled, with a luminous, mnemonic clarity that amazed me, a long-ago day when he virtually predicted my presence on a ship like the USS *General Washburn*, making its cumbersome passage to the outlandish coast of Okinawa . . .

The title of the story in *The Saturday Evening Post* was "The Curse of the Rising Sun," and I was reading it in the back of the family Oldsmobile, broken down with engine trouble beside a peanut field near the Virginia-Carolina line. At eleven I could read *Post* fiction with contemptuous ease, but I was not quite old enough to avoid being troubled by the fantasy—a 1930s version of spy thriller spiced up with a touch of futuristic horror. In the front seat my mother, her leg in a steel brace, gazed stolidly forward through the fading light of an October afternoon while my father labored over the steaming engine. I was the classic only child—snotty, self-absorbed—and I offered neither solace nor help,

curled up in the back with my chronicle of the nightmare that engulfed America "in the early 1950s." It was
untethered hell. Colossal submarines the size of ocean
liners had disgorged their weasel-faced hordes at a
dozen landing sites from Seattle to San Diego. Paralysis
had ensued as the nation failed to mobilize its defenses.
California had become another Manchuria, prostrate, in
thrall. San Francisco lay pillaged, the people destroyed
like insects. Feeble resistance had allowed Los Angeles
to be overrun; the palaces of the movie moguls were
occupied by smirking officers, rattling their samurai
swords and defiling starlets. (I remember one captioned
line drawing: *"I saw your film in Tokyo,"* said Colonel
*Oishi sneeringly to the cringing Gloria. "A pretty dance.
Now you will perform for me another kind of dance."*) As
Part One began to wind down (I peeked ahead and
discovered that "The Curse of the Rising Sun" was a
serial in three segments), a certain Major Bradshaw of
U.S. Army Intelligence, based with the Defense Command in Denver, spoke on the telephone to his wife
back east, imparting the news that the Imperial Fifth
Army, a legion of fiends specializing in babies and old
people, was advancing across the Arizona desert toward
Phoenix, where her parents lived. She sobbed; he coun-
seled courage. Troops from Texas were on the way.
Continued next week.

There was a thick cloud of rage in and around our
stalled car. For good reason, we were not a very happy
little family. But we generally kept our tempers and

were decent with one another, being well-bred and imbued with many of the more gentle Christian prescriptions. Indeed, our love for one another had a special desperation. But I could almost hear the rage humming in the warm autumn air. My father, a patient man, was enraged because he could not fix the engine; he was a graduate of North Carolina State College, an engineering school, and never could reconcile this with his mechanical incompetence. Essentially he was a poet who had stumbled by error into technology. I heard him whispering his Presbyterian curses: "Blast it! Jeru-sa-*lem*!" My mother was in a quiet, stony rage because the night before at my grandmother's house in Carolina, whence we were returning, I had misbehaved, and had misbehaved again in the car, making some brattish remarks about all the niggers in that part of the country, which caused her to cry out, in words I had never heard her use before: "Shut your mouth!" I was in a rage because of my guilt over the word I'd said, yet ego-stung and enraged at her rage. By demoralizingly slow and painful degrees she was being killed by cancer, and this too was part of the overall rage we felt. I was supposed to be unaware of her condition, formally, but wondered why, since I was neither stupid nor blind. A minor crisis other people would greet with a show of humor or equanimity made my mother and father, and eventually me, become frazzled and exhausted because of the way it represented in microcosm the oncoming disaster none of us could face or bear.

Sulky, halfhearted, I tried to restore a touch of good-will. I said: "In about fifteen years the Japanese are going to be in the United States, and we're going to be fighting them."

My mother was silent. When she spoke, a soft undertone told me that she had curbed her anger at me; she had always been blunt, though, and now she said what was on her mind. "Paul, you've been reading that ridiculous story in the *Post.* Your father subscribes to that magazine, though I don't know why. That story's simply trash. It's also dripping with racial prejudice." My mother was a cum laude Bryn Mawr graduate, high-principled, shrewd, and liberated; a Pennsylvania Yankee, she wore her abolitionism like a badge of honor in this part of the Tidewater, an enclave of ancient counties as fanatically segregated as darkest Alabama. "One of my dearest friends, Annie Wardlaw, whom you never knew—she died—lived for a long time in Japan with her husband, who was a diplomat. She loved the Japanese. They're not like those—those *beasts* in that magazine. A story like that is *inflammatory.*"

I remember asking what "inflammatory" meant. I gazed out at the peanut-field-and-pine-grove monotony of the landscape, the potholed asphalt highway down which, toward us, now came an incredible rattletrap of a truck, swaying and top-heavy with a dozen farm Negroes in overalls and the homemade, patched and repatched Mother Hubbards of those destitute years. It slowly crept past us, the motor stuttering, its human cargo a jumble of rolling eyeballs and flashing teeth and agitated wavings and jumpings. "Does you need any help?" I heard the driver call out. But I could sense that this only added fuel to my father's fury as he nodded them on their way.

" 'Inflammatory,' " my mother said, "is an adjective to describe that ugly word you used ten minutes ago about these people you see here in this countryside. A word like that is inflammatory. And disgusting."

She was unfair. She had already upbraided me violently; now she had recommenced the attack. Her unfairness began to restore my rage. Whatever I was on the verge of saying in protest was cut off by my father, who flung open the door and sank down behind the steering wheel in despair. "I don't know what's wrong! The distributor. A short. I don't know! There's not a telephone for miles!" His hands were black, greasy, quivering with tension.

"Why didn't you let those Negroes help you?" my mother said.

"Daddy," I heard myself saying, "the Japanese are going to invade the United States." Inside me there was an intense need for retaliation, so I then employed a touch of the magazine story's straight-shooting vocabulary. "Bunch of slimy butchers."

"You stop that kind of language!" she exclaimed, stirring to turn around and face me, in a jerky movement that must have caused her pain. "We are not going to war with anyone!" She glanced at my father.

"Why do you read that magazine? Why do you consciously expose an eleven-year-old to such garbage?"

"Listen, Adelaide, they have printed that genius from Mississippi, William Faulkner," he said, making a fatigued sound. "And one of your favorites, F. Scott Fitzgerald. Also clever escape fiction like the story in question."

"There's something profoundly immoral about publishing scare stories about war," my mother retorted, "especially when they can be read by some children."

"Scare stories about war!" he echoed her mockingly. "How can you be so idiotic? I hate to say this, but I think you're an idealistic *fool.* You ought to have your head examined!"

I was stupefied. The words had thrust a dagger through my chest. His dignity and forbearance had been such an abiding part of his nature that tones like these seemed—there was no other word—monstrous. Please! I had never once heard him lift his voice to my mother; her affliction had caused him to bestow on her daily an almost reverential tenderness. But now—this fury. It may have been only his aggregate frustrations—the sick engine, his family stranded in a backwoods nowhere, the bickering, my misbehavior, some unfocused anxiety. Whatever, he began to harangue my mother with a bully's scorn. His manner sickened me. At first she flinched as if he had hit her; then she drew back and stared at him as if he had gone crazy.

"Adelaide, don't you realize the whole world is

aflame with war—has been, is, and ever will be? What do you think I've been doing with myself these past years? What do you think I helped build the *Ranger* for? To send airplanes sightseeing over Chesapeake Bay? What do you think we've built the *Yorktown* for? And the *Enterprise*. And why do you think we'll be building the *Hornet*? And so on ad infinitum. Do you think the United States government is spending millions of dollars on these ships just to have a handsome, up-to-date, show-off Navy? No, my dear"—the "dear," usually so gentle, had a hard, sardonic tone—"they are to make war, and they will make war and you and I and all our friends on the Virginia Peninsula even now are the beneficiaries. Are you so blind that you can't see the contradiction of this awful poverty over here in Nansemond County, while we ride in an Oldsmobile—a defective Oldsmobile, as we have seen demonstrated, but the kind of car that very few people are privileged to ride in, in the midst of economic collapse. It is simple, my dear. We are the lucky few feeding off profits made from the machinery of warfare." He paused for an instant, then said: "And what about those Flying Fortresses from Langley Field, Addy, and their racket you complain about nearly every morning? Do you think they're merely part of some game we're playing? And the Navy fighter planes from Norfolk? And the minelayers from Yorktown? And those truck convoys rolling down every day from Fort Eustis? Certainly all that has to be put to use! Don't you see—"

Suddenly he came to a halt. Knowing my father as well as I did, I sensed there was no way he could long sustain this harsh, aggressive mood. And indeed at that very moment he turned away from my mother and looked straight ahead down the highway, at the same time raising his hand to touch consoling fingers against her shoulder. I saw her relax again; the perplexity and momentary shock softened, faded into a pale calm, and I relaxed too, feeling the hunched-up muscles in my arms and legs go limp with relief.

"Oh, Lord, forgive me, Addy," he said at last, in a distant grieving voice. "I'm sorry to raise my voice like that. But I can't help thinking"—again he hesitated, as if searching for words, and for what seemed a long while the only sound in the car was that of our breathing, a trio of different rhythms—"I can't help thinking of the *generations*—as I once told you, I think: every direct ancestor hurt or mutilated or dead in nearly all the wars this country has fought. The great-grandfathers in the Revolution and in 1812. Both of them scarred. My grandfather in that despicable war with Mexico, dead at Buena Vista. My own father at the age of seventeen half-blinded and mutilated so badly at Chancellorsville that he hobbled and jerked like a spastic for the rest of his life. I alone got away during the Great War because of that friendly heart murmur, but somehow compensated for this by serving my apprenticeship in the shipyard, building heavy cruisers." He turned to her briefly. "I suppose you could say that it was your poor brother David who, in a distant and indirect sense, kept it in the family, became my substitute, his mind blown away at Château-Thierry, so that even now, wandering around that veterans hospital at Perry Point——"

"Don't," she whispered, and slowly let her head fall against the back of the seat. She was not yet fifty. Years before, beyond the limit of my earliest memory, her hair had turned gray, and now most of it was white, though remarkably soft and lustrous because of her determination to keep a trace of her former beauty. It reminded me of the white of gardenias, and now the glossy strands of it next to her brow had become damp and darkened with tears. "Don't say any more, please," she said.

It was plain that he was ravaged inside by what he had caused himself to spill forth. He had also (I think unwittingly) allowed a meditation on war to flow to the edge of an unspoken thought——a prophecy concerning his only son and heir. As always, as much as I adored him, I was embarrassed by the emotionalism that impelled him, with passion at once fierce and clumsy, to twist around and with both arms embrace my head and my mother's as if trying to merge them into one, murmuring: "Dearly beloved . . . dearly beloved."

Even as Halloran's words broke through the cloak of memory, broke through my whiskey haze, I was aware that he had neared the end of a story he had told us before. Stiles and I gazed patiently at the colonel, who drifted back to stage center. He was poised delightedly at the edge of his denouement. The teeth flashed beneath the vaudeville mustache and the laughter heaving up from his chest had made him very nearly incoherent. "So Willie," he gasped, "so Willie was lying there with this broad Ludmilla. They still had their clothes on, you see, but he knew for sure he was going to score. And then he got his hand down there—you know where—and she was moaning and groaning and suddenly he felt"—another gasp—"and suddenly he felt what was obviously this big, stiff . . . Russian . . . *gazoo*!"

Counterfeiting laughter with convincing heartiness is another of my social skills, and I joined with Stiles in the general explosion of merriment. "Oh, wow!" I cried.

"It wasn't a *she*, this Ludmilla, you see, but a *he*. He was a White Russian fruitcake, I mean one of those whattayoucallems—"

"A drag queen," Stiles put in, "a transvestite?"

"Yeah, that's it. Boy, did Willie make tracks out of that joint!"

Our laughter died away but amid the residue of chuckles Halloran fell into thought. "Willie almost never got over that, but it was quite a story." A tone of gravity crept in. "Jesus, though, imagine what he must have felt like afterwards. I mean, think of *kissing*. Having your tongue inside the mouth of this Igor or Boris or whatever the fuck his name must have been." He gave a shudder. "Murder!"

"Make you sick to your stomach just thinking about it," Stiles said accommodatingly.

"What in the goddamned hell are you crying for, Paul?" I suddenly heard Halloran say, shocking me back into present time. On one's face the borderline between hilarity and grief may be, of course, ill-defined; thus I was able to press one hand against my brow, concealing my eyes while I murmured, "So funny, so funny," and let the tears of sorrow continue to course down my cheeks. In reality the homesickness that had first seized me when I awoke on deck had now engulfed my spirit, and I felt as helpless and as vulnerable as I had at any time since I had gone to war. I'm sure the remembrance of my father's desolation had made me sense the power of history to utterly victimize humanity, composed of forgettable ciphers like myself. What am I doing in this strange fucking horrible war? I thought, dumbfounded by the virginal freshness of the question I posed to myself. I rose from the bunk and quickly mumbled an excuse, saying that I had to go to the head, but once clear of the cabin I plunged down the putrid-smelling passageway in the opposite direction and burst out again onto the deck. I hung over the rail for a while, and let the cathartic tears drip, windblown, into the sea. After the unnumbered hours and days I had trained for warfare, I perceived the first small chink in the armor of my bravado; I accepted the sweet logic of the inner voice telling me: *You are really grateful that you won't be invading that island tomorrow; you will be overjoyed to go back to Saipan.* Then I banished the treacherous advocate from my mind, wiped my eyes, and stalked back to the cabin through clots and clumps of Marines who were oiling their rifles and making their unsheathed bayonets glitter like spears. "Is it true, sir," I heard one kid say, "that they're goin' to pull the plug on us? Is it true that we're not ever going to make a landing?"

"Sir, is what we hear true?" called another. "That we're goin' to head back to Saipan without seein' any action?"

"I honestly can't say," I called back. "If it's true, then, boys, we're getting a royal screwing."

I actually shivered at the insincerity that gripped me as I spoke these words: their falseness was shameful. I was sure my coolness would return. I'd just been caught with my guard down. But at the moment I was in shambles. Walking along the deck (adopting my old casual swagger), I jollied up the troops with small talk, put on a frozen grin, and kept murmuring to myself with rhythmic fatuity: *You love the Marine Corps, it's a terrific war, you love the Marine Corps, it's a terrific war . . .*

Shadrach

My tenth summer on earth, in the year 1935, will never leave my mind because of Shadrach and the way he brightened and darkened my life then and thereafter. He turned up as if from nowhere, arriving at high noon in the village where I grew up in Tidewater Virginia. He was a black apparition of unbelievable antiquity, palsied and feeble, blue-gummed and grinning, a caricature of a caricature at a time when every creaky, superannuated Negro grandsire was (in the eyes of society, not alone the eyes of a small southern white boy) a combination of Stepin Fetchit and Uncle Remus. On that day when he seemed to materialize before us, almost out of the ether, we were playing marbles. Little boys rarely play marbles nowadays but marbles were an obsession in 1935, somewhat predating the yo-yo as a kids' craze. One could admire these elegant many-colored spheres as potentates admire rubies and emeralds; they had a sound yet slippery substantiality, evoking the tactile delight——the same aesthetic yet opulent plea-sure——of small precious globes of jade. Thus, among other things, my memory of Shadrach is bound up with the lapidary feel of marbles in my fingers and the odor of cool bare earth on a smoldering hot day beneath a sycamore tree, and still another odor (ineffably a part of the moment): a basic fetor which that squeamish decade christened B.O., and which radiated from a child named Little Mole Dabney, my opponent at marbles. He was ten years old, too, and had never been known to use Lifebuoy soap, or any other cleansing agent.

Which brings me soon enough to the Dabneys. For I realize I must deal with the Dabneys in order to try to explain the encompassing mystery of Shadrach—who after a fashion was a Dabney himself. The Dabneys were not close neighbors; they lived nearby down the road in a rambling weatherworn house that lacked a lawn. On the grassless, graceless terrain of the front yard was a random litter of eviscerated Frigidaires, electric generators, stoves, and the remains of two or three ancient automobiles, whose scavenged carcasses lay abandoned beneath the sycamores like huge rusted insects. Poking up through these husks were masses of weeds and hollyhocks, dandelions gone to seed, sunflowers. Junk and auto parts were a sideline of Mr. Dabney's. He also did odd jobs, but his primary pursuit was bootlegging.

Like such noble Virginia family names as Randolph and Peyton and Tucker and Harrison and Lee and Fitzhugh and a score of others, the patronym Dabney is an illustrious one, but with the present Dabney, christened Vernon, the name had lost almost all of its luster. He should have gone to the University of Virginia; instead, he dropped out of school in the fifth grade. It was not his fault; nor was it his fault that the family had so declined in status. It was said that his father (a true scion of the distinguished old tree but a man with a character defect and a weakness for the bottle) had long ago slid down the social ladder, forfeiting his F.F.V. status by marrying a half-breed Mattaponi or Pamunkey Indian girl from the York River, which accounted perhaps for the black hair and sallowish muddy complexion of the son.

Mr. Dabney—at this time, I imagine he was in his forties—was a runty, hyperactive entrepreneur with a sourly intense, purse-lipped, preoccupied air and a sometimes rampaging temper. He also had a ridiculously foul mouth, from which I learned my first dirty words. It was with delectation, with the same sickishly delighted apprehension of evil that beset me about eight years later when I was accosted by my first prostitute, that I heard Mr. Dabney in his frequent transports of rage use those words forbidden to me in my own home. His blasphemies and obscenities, far from scaring me, caused me to shiver with their splendor. I practiced his words in secret, deriving from their amalgamated filth what, in a dim pediatric way, I could perceive was erotic inflammation. "Son of a bitch whorehouse bat shit Jesus Christ pisspot asshole!" I would screech into an empty closet, and feel my little ten-year-old pecker rise. Yet as ugly and threatening as Mr. Dabney might sometimes appear, I was never really daunted by him, for he had a humane and gentle side. Although he might curse like a stevedore at his wife and children, at the assorted mutts and cats that thronged the place, at the pet billy goat, which he once caught in the act of devouring his new three-dollar Thom McAn shoes, I soon saw that even his most murderous fits were largely bluster. This would include his loud and eccentric dislike of Franklin D. Roosevelt. Most down-and-out people of the Tidewater revered F.D.R., like poor people everywhere; not Mr. Dabney. Much later I surmised that his tantrums probably derived from a pining to return to his aristocratic origins.

Oh, how I loved the Dabneys! I actually wanted to *be* a Dabney—wanted to change my name from Paul Whitehurst to Paul Dabney. I visited the Dabney homestead as often as I could, basking in its casual squalor. I must avoid giving the impression of Tobacco Road; the Dabneys were of better quality. Yet there were similarities. The mother, named Trixie, was a huge sweaty generous sugarloaf of a woman, often drunk. It was she, I am sure, who propagated the domestic sloppiness. But I loved her passionately, just as I loved and envied the whole Dabney tribe and that total absence in them of the bourgeois aspirations and gentility which were my own inheritance. I envied the sheer teeming multitude of the Dabneys—there were seven children—which made my status as an only child seem so effete, spoiled, and lonesome. Only illicit whiskey kept the family from complete destitution, and I envied their near poverty. Also their religion. They were Baptists: as a Presbyterian I envied that. To be totally immersed—how wet and natural! They lived in a house devoid of books or any reading matter except funny papers—more envy. I envied their abandoned slovenliness, their sour unmade beds, their roaches, the cracked linoleum on the floor, the homely cur dogs leprous with mange that foraged at will through house and yard. My perverse longings were—to turn around a phrase unknown at the time—downwardly mobile. Afflicted at the age of ten by *nostalgie de la boue,* I felt deprived of a certain depravity. I was too young to know, of course, that one of the countless things of which the Dabneys were victims was the Great Depression.

Yet beneath this scruffy façade, the Dabneys were a family of some property. Although their ramshackle house was rented, as were most of the dwellings in our village, they owned a place elsewhere, and there was occasionally chatter in the household about "the Farm," far upriver in King and Queen County. Mr. Dabney had inherited the place from his dissolute father and it had been in the family for generations. It could not have been much of a holding, or else it would have been sold years before, and when, long afterward, I came to absorb the history of the Virginia Tidewater—that primordial American demesne where the land was sucked dry by tobacco, laid waste and destroyed a whole century before golden California became an idea, much less a hope or a westward dream—I realized that the Dabney farm must have been as nondescript and as pathetic a relic as any of the scores of shrunken, abandoned "plantations" scattered for a hundred miles across the tidelands between the Potomac and the James. The chrysalis, unpainted, of a dinky, thrice-rebuilt farmhouse with a few mean acres in corn and second-growth timber—that was all. Nonetheless it was to this ancestral dwelling that the nine Dabneys, packed like squirming eels into a fifteen-year-old Model T Ford pockmarked with the ulcers of terminal decay, would go forth for a month's sojourn each August, as seemingly bland and blasé about their customary estivation as Rockefellers decamping to Pocantico Hills. But they were not entirely vacationing. I did not know then but discovered later that the woodland glens and lost glades of the depopulated land of King and Queen were every moonshiner's dream for hideaways in which to decoct white lightning, and the exodus to "the Farm" served a purpose beyond the purely recreative: each Dabney, of whatever age and sex, had at least a hand in the operation of the still, even if it was simply shucking corn.

All of the three Dabney boys bore the nickname Mole, being differentiated from each other by a logical nomenclature—Little, Middle, and Big Mole; I don't think I ever knew their real names. It was the youngest of the three Moles I was playing marbles with when Shadrach made his appearance. Little Mole was a child of stunning ugliness, sharing with his brothers an inherited mixture of bulging thyroid eyes, mashed-in spoonlike nose, and jutting jaw that (I say in retrospect) might have nicely corresponded to Cesare Lombroso's description of the criminal physiognomy. Something more remarkable—accounting surely for their collective nickname—was the fact that save for their graduated sizes they were nearly exact replicas of each other, appearing related less as brothers than as monotonous clones, as if Big Mole had reproduced Middle, who in turn had created Little, my evil-smelling playmate. None of the Moles ever wished or was ever required to bathe, and this accounted for another phenomenon. At the vast and dismal consolidated rural school we attended, one could mark the presence of any of the three Dabney brothers in a classroom by the ring of empty desks isolating each Mole from his classmates, who, edging away without apology from the effluvium, would leave the poor Mole abandoned in his aloneness, like some species of bacterium on a microscope slide whose noxious discharge has destroyed all life in a circle around it.

By contrast—the absurdity of genetics!—the four Dabney girls were fair, fragrant in their Woolworth perfumes, buxom, lusciously ripe of hindquarter, at least two of them knocked up and wed before attaining full growth. Oh, those lost beauties . . .

That day Little Mole took aim with a glittering taw of surreal chalcedony; he had warts on his fingers, his odor in my nostrils was quintessential Mole. He sent my agate spinning into the weeds.

Shadrach appeared then. We somehow sensed his presence, looked up, and found him there. We had not

heard him approach; he had come as silently and por-
tentously as if he had been lowered on some celestial
apparatus operated by unseen hands. He was astound-
ingly black. I had never seen a Negro of that impenetra-
ble hue: it was blackness of such intensity that it
reflected no light at all, achieving a virtual obliteration
of facial features and taking on a mysterious undertone
that had the blue-gray of ashes. Perched on a fender, he
was grinning at us from the rusted frame of a demol-
ished Pierce-Arrow. It was a blissful grin, which re-
vealed deathly purple gums, the yellowish stumps of
two teeth, and a wet mobile tongue. For a long while he
said nothing but, continuing to grin, contentedly rooted
at his crotch with a hand warped and wrinkled with
age: the bones moved beneath the black skin in clear
skeletal outline. With his other hand he firmly grasped
a walking stick.

It was then that I felt myself draw a breath in wonder at his age, which was surely unfathomable. He
looked older than all the patriarchs of Genesis whose
names flooded my mind in a Sunday school litany:
Lamech, Noah, Enoch, and that perdurable old Jewish
fossil Methuselah. Little Mole and I drew closer, and I
saw then that the old man had to be at least partially
blind; cataracts clouded his eyes like milky cauls, the
corneas swam with rheum. Yet he was not entirely
without sight. I sensed the way he observed our approach; above the implacable sweet grin there were
flickers of wise recognition. His presence remained wor-

risomely biblical; I felt myself drawn to him with an almost devout compulsion, as if he were the prophet Elijah sent to bring truth, light, the Word. The shiny black mohair mail-order suit he wore was baggy and frayed, streaked with dust; the cuffs hung loose, and from one of the ripped ankle-high clodhoppers protruded a naked black toe. Even so, the presence was thrillingly ecclesiastical and fed my piety.

It was midsummer. The very trees seemed to hover on the edge of combustion; a mockingbird began to chant nearby in notes rippling and clear. I walked closer to the granddaddy through a swarm of fat green flies supping hungrily on the assorted offal carpeting the Dabney yard. Streams of sweat were pouring off the ancient black face. Finally I heard him speak, in a senescent voice so faint and garbled that it took moments for it to penetrate my understanding. But I understood: "Praise de Lawd. Praise his sweet name! Ise arrived in Ole Virginny!"

He beckoned to me with one of his elongated, bony, bituminous fingers; at first it alarmed me but then the finger seemed to move appealingly, like a small harmless snake. "Climb up on ole Shad's knee," he said. I was beginning to get the hang of his gluey diction, realized that it was a matter of listening to certain internal rhythms; even so, with the throaty gulping sound of Africa in it, it was nigger talk I had never heard before. "Jes climb up," he commanded. I obeyed. I obeyed with love and eagerness; it was like creeping up against the bosom of Abraham. In the collapsed old lap I sat happily, fingering a brass chain which wound across the grease-shiny vest; at the end of the chain, dangling, was a nickel-plated watch upon the face of which the black mitts of Mickey Mouse marked the noontime hour. Giggling now, snuggled against the ministerial breast, I inhaled the odor of great age—indefinable, not exactly unpleasant but stale, like a long-unopened cupboard—mingled with the smell of unlaundered fabric and dust. Only inches away the tongue quivered like a pink clapper in the dark gorge of a cavernous bell. "You jes a sweetie," he crooned. "Is you a Dabney?" I replied with regret, "No," and pointed to Little Mole. "That's a Dabney," I said.

"You a sweetie, too," he said, summoning Little Mole with the outstretched forefinger, black, palsied, wiggling. "Oh, you jes de sweetest thing!" The voice rose joyfully. Little Mole looked perplexed. I felt Shadrach's entire body quiver; to my mystification he was overcome with emotion at beholding a flesh-and-blood Dabney, and as he reached toward the boy I heard him breathe again: "Praise de Lawd! Ise arrived in Ole Virginny!"

Then at that instant Shadrach suffered a cataclysmic crisis—one that plainly had to do with the fearful heat. He could not, of course, grow pallid, but something enormous and vital did dissolve within the black eternity of his face; the wrinkled old skin of his cheeks sagged, his milky eyes rolled blindly upward, and uttering a soft moan, he fell back across the car's ruptured seat with its naked springs and its holes disgorging horsehair.

"Watah!" I heard him cry feebly, *"Watah!"* I slid out of his lap, watched the scrawny black legs no bigger around than pine saplings begin to shake and twitch. "Watah, please!" I heard the voice implore, but Little Mole and I needed no further urging; we were gone— racing headlong to the kitchen and the cluttered, reeking sink. "That old cullud man's dying!" Little Mole wailed. We got a cracked jelly glass, ran water from the faucet in a panic, speculating as we did: Little Mole ventured the notion of a heat stroke; I theorized a heart attack. We screamed and babbled; we debated whether the water should be at body temperature or iced. Little Mole added half a cupful of salt, then decided that the water should be hot. Our long delay was fortunate, for several moments later, as we hurried with the terrible potion to Shadrach's side, we found that the elder Dabney had appeared from a far corner of the yard and, taking command of the emergency, had pried Shadrach away from the seat of the Pierce-Arrow, dragged or carried him across the plot of bare earth, propped him up against a tree trunk, and now stood sluicing water from a garden hose into Shadrach's gaping mouth. The old man gulped his fill. Then Mr. Dabney, small and fiercely intent in his baggy overalls, hunched down over the stricken patriarch, whipped out a pint bottle from his pocket, and poured a stream of crystalline whiskey down Shadrach's gorge. While he did this he muttered to himself in tones of incredulity and inwardly tickled amazement: "Well, kiss my ass! Who are you, old uncle? Just who in the goddamned hell *are* you?"

We heard Shadrach give a strangled cough; then he began to try out something resembling speech. But the word he was almost able to produce was swallowed and lost in the hollow of his throat.

"What did he say? What did he say?" Mr. Dabney demanded impatiently.

"He said his name is Shadrach!" I shouted, proud that I alone seemed able to fathom this obscure Negro dialect, further muddied by the crippled cadences of senility.

"What's he want, Paul?" Mr. Dabney said to me.

I bent my face toward Shadrach's, which looked contented again. His voice in my ear was at once whispery and sweet, a gargle of beatitude: "Die on Dabney ground."

"I think he said," I told Mr. Dabney at last, "that he wants to die on Dabney ground."

"Well, I'll be goddamned," said Mr. Dabney.

"Praise de Lawd!" Shadrach cried suddenly, in a voice that even Mr. Dabney could understand. "Ise arrived in Ole Virginny!"

Mr. Dabney roared at me: "Ask him where he came from!"

Again I inclined my face to that black shrunken visage upturned to the blazing sun; I whispered the question and the reply came back after a long silence, in fitful stammerings. At last I said to Mr. Dabney: "He says he's from Clay County down in Alabama."

"*Alabama!* Well, kiss my ass!"

I felt Shadrach pluck at my sleeve and once more I bent down to listen. Many seconds passed before I could discover the outlines of the words struggling for meaning on the flailing, ungovernable tongue. But finally I captured their shapes, arranged them in order.

"What did he say now, Paul?" Mr. Dabney said.

"He said he wants you to bury him."

"*Bury him!*" Mr. Dabney shouted. "How can I bury him? He ain't even dead yet!"

From Shadrach's breast there now came a gentle keening sound which, commencing on a note of the purest grief, startled me by the way it resolved itself suddenly into a mild faraway chuckle; the moonshine was taking hold. The pink clapper of a tongue lolled in the cave of the jagged old mouth. Shadrach grinned.

"Ask him how old he is, Paul," came the command. I asked him. "Nimenime" was the glutinous reply.

"He says he's ninety-nine years old," I reported, glancing up from the ageless abyss.

"*Ninety-nine!* Well, I'll be goddamned!"

Now other Dabneys began to arrive, including the mother, Trixie, and the two larger Moles, along with one of the older teenage daughters, whalelike but meltingly beautiful as she floated on the crest of her pregnancy, and accompanied by her hulking, acne-cratered teenage spouse. There also came a murmuring clutch of neighbors—sun-reddened shipyard workers in cheap sport shirts, scampering towhead children, a quartet of scrawny housewives in sacklike dresses, bluish crescents of sweat beneath their arms. In my memory they make an aching tableau of those exhausted years. They jabbered and clucked in wonder at Shadrach, who, immobilized by alcohol, heat, infirmity, and his ninety-nine Augusts, beamed and raised his rheumy eyes to the sun. "Praise de Lawd!" he quavered.

We hoisted him to his feet and supported the frail, almost weightless old frame as he limped on dancing tiptoe to the house, where we settled him down upon a rumpsprung glider that squatted on the back porch in an ambient fragrance of dog urine, tobacco smoke, and mildew. "You hungry, Shad?" Mr. Dabney bellowed. "Mama, get Shadrach something to eat!" Slumped in the glider, the ancient visitor gorged himself like one plucked from the edge of critical starvation: he devoured three cantaloupes, slurped down bowl after bowl of Rice Krispies, and gummed his way through a panful of hot cornbread smeared with lard. We watched silently, in wonderment. Before our solemnly attentive eyes he gently and carefully eased himself back on the malodorous pillows and with a soft sigh went to sleep.

Some time after this—during the waning hours of the afternoon, when Shadrach woke up, and then on into the evening—the mystery of the old man's appearance became gradually unlocked. One of the Dabney daughters was a fawn-faced creature of twelve named Edmonia; her fragile beauty (especially when contrasted with ill-favored brothers) and her precocious breasts and bottom had caused me—young as I was—a troubling, unresolved itch. I was awed by the ease and nonchalance with which she wiped the drool from Shadrach's lips. Like me, she possessed some inborn gift of interpretation, and through our joint efforts there was pieced together over several hours an explanation for this old man—for his identity and his bizarre and inescapable coming.

He stayed on the glider; we put another pillow under his head. Nourishing his dragon's appetite with Hershey bars and, later on, with nips from Mr. Dabney's bottle, we were able to coax from those aged lips a fragmented, abbreviated, but reasonably coherent biography. After a while it became an anxious business for, as one of the adults noticed, old Shad seemed to be running a fever; his half-blind eyes swam about from time to time, and the clotted phlegm that rose in his throat made it all the more difficult to understand anything. But somehow we began to divine the truth. One phrase, repeated over and over, I particularly remember: "Ise a Dabney." And indeed those words provided the chief clue to his story.

Born a slave on the Dabney plantation in King and Queen County, he had been sold down to Alabama in the decades before the Civil War. Shadrach's memory was imperfect regarding the date of his sale. Once he said "fifty," meaning 1850, and another time he said "fifty-five," but it was an item of little importance; he was probably somewhere between fifteen and twenty-five years old when his master—Vernon Dabney's great-grandfather—disposed of him, selling him to one of the many traders prowling the worn-out Virginia soil of that stricken bygone era; and since in his confessional to us, garbled as it was, he used the word "coffle" (a word beyond my ten-year-old knowledge but one whose meaning I later understood), he must have journeyed those six hundred miles to Alabama on foot and in the company of God knows how many other black slaves, linked together by chains.

So now, as we began slowly to discover, this was Shadrach's return trip home to Ole Virginny—three quarters of a century or thereabouts after his departure from the land out of which he had sprung, which had nurtured him, and where he had lived his happy years. Happy? Who knows? But we had to assume they were his happy years—else why this incredible pilgrimage at the end of his life? As he had announced with such abrupt fervor earlier, he wanted only to die and be buried on "Dabney ground."

We learned that after the war he had become a sharecropper, that he had married three times and had had many children (once he said twelve, another time fifteen; no matter, they were legion); he had outlived them all, wives and offspring. Even the grandchildren had died off, or had somehow vanished. "Ah was divested of all mah plenty" was another statement I can still record verbatim. Thus divested and (as he cheerfully made plain to all who gathered around him to listen) sensing mortality in his own shriveled flesh and bones, he had departed Alabama on foot—just as he had come there—to find the Virginia of his youth.

Six hundred miles! The trip, we were able to gather, took over four months, since he said he set out from Clay County in the early spring. He walked nearly the entire way, although now and then he would accept a ride—almost always, one can be sure, from the few Negroes who owned cars in the rural South of those years. He had saved up a few dollars, which allowed him to provide for his stomach. He slept on the side of the road or in barns; sometimes a friendly Negro family would give him shelter. The trek took him across Georgia and the Carolinas and through Southside Virginia. His itinerary is still anyone's conjecture. Because he could not read either road sign or road map, he obviously followed his own northward-questing nose, a profoundly imperfect method of finding one's way (he allowed to Edmonia with a faint cackle), since he once got so far astray that he ended up not only miles away from the proper highway but in a city and state completely off his route—Chattanooga, Tennessee. But he circled back and moved on. And how, once arrived in Virginia with its teeming Dabneys, did he discover the only Dabney who would matter, the single Dabney who was not merely the proprietor of his birthplace but the one whom he also unquestioningly expected to oversee his swiftly approaching departure, laying him to rest in the earth of their mutual ancestors? How did he find *Vernon Dabney*? Mr. Dabney was by no means an ill-spirited or ungenerous man (despite his runaway temper), but was a soul nonetheless beset by many woes in the dingy threadbare year 1935, being hard pressed not merely for dollars but for dimes and quarters, crushed beneath an elephantine and inebriate wife, along with three generally shiftless sons and two knocked-up daughters, plus two more likely to be so, and living with the abiding threat of revenue agents swooping down to terminate his livelihood and, perhaps, get him sent to the Atlanta penitentiary for five or six years. He needed no more cares or burdens, and now in the hot katydid-shrill hours of summer night I saw him gaze down at the leathery old dying black face with an expression that mingled compassion and bewilderment and stoppered-up rage and desperation, and then whisper to himself: "He wants to die on Dabney ground! Well, kiss my ass, just kiss my ass!" Plainly he wondered how, among all his horde of Virginia kinfolk, Shadrach found *him*, for he squatted low and murmured: "Shad! Shad, how come you knew who to look for?" But in his fever Shadrach had drifted off to sleep, and so far as I ever knew there was never any answer to that.

• • •

The next day it was plain that Shadrach was badly off. During the night he had somehow fallen from the glider, and in the early morning hours he was discovered on the floor, leaking blood. We bandaged him up. The wound just above his ear was superficial, as it turned out, but it had done him no good; and when he was replaced on the swing he appeared to be confused and at the edge of delirium, plucking at his shirt, whispering, and rolling his gentle opaque eyes at the ceiling. Whenever he spoke now, his words were beyond the power of Edmonia or me to comprehend, faint high-pitched mumbo jumbo in a drowned dialect. He seemed to recognize no one. Trixie, leaning over the old man as she sucked at her first Pabst Blue Ribbon of the morning, decided firmly that there was no time to waste. "Shoog," she said to Mr. Dabney, using her habitual pet name (diminutive form of Sugar), "you better get out the car if we're goin' to the Farm. I think he ain't gone last much longer." And so, given unusual parental leave to go along on the trip, I squeezed myself into the backseat of the Model T, privileged to hold in my lap a huge greasy paper bag full of fried chicken which Trixie had prepared for noontime dinner at the Farm.

Not all of the Dabneys made the journey—the two older daughters and the largest Mole were left behind—but we still composed a multitude. We children were packed sweatily skin to skin and atop each other's laps in the rear seat, which reproduced in miniature the messiness of the house with this new litter of empty RC

Cola and Nehi bottles, funny papers, watermelon rinds, banana peels, greasy jack handles, oil-smeared gears of assorted sizes, and wads of old Kleenex. On the floor beneath my feet I even discerned (to my intense discomfort, for I had just learned to recognize such an object) a crumpled, yellowish used condom, left there haphazardly, I was certain, by one of the older daughters' boyfriends who had been able to borrow the heap for carnal sport. It was a bright summer day, scorchingly hot like the day preceding it, but the car had no workable windows and we were pleasantly ventilated. Shadrach sat in the middle of the front seat. Mr. Dabney was hunched over the wheel, chewing at a wad of tobacco and driving with black absorption; he had stripped to his undershirt, and I thought I could almost see the rage and frustration in the tight bunched muscles of his neck. He muttered curses at the balky gearshift but otherwise said little, rapt in his guardian misery. So voluminous that the flesh of her shoulders fell in a freckled cascade over the back of her seat, Trixie loomed on the other side of Shadrach; the corpulence of her body seemed in some way to both enfold and support the old man, who nodded and dozed. The encircling hair around the shiny black head was, I thought, like a delicate halo of the purest frost or foam. Curiously, for the first time since Shadrach's coming, I felt a stab of grief and achingly wanted him not to die.

"Shoog," said Trixie, standing by the rail of the dumpy little ferry that crossed the York River, "what kind of big birds do you reckon those are behind that boat there?" The Model T had been the first car aboard, and all of us had flocked out to look at the river, leaving Shadrach to sit there and sleep during the fifteen-minute ride. The water was blue, sparkling with whitecaps, lovely. A huge gray naval tug with white markings chugged along to the mine depot at Yorktown, trailing eddies of garbage and a swooping flock of frantic gulls. Their squeals echoed across the peaceful channel.

"Seagulls," said Mr. Dabney. "Ain't you never recognized seagulls before? I can't believe such a question. Seagulls. Dumb greedy bastards."

"Beautiful things," she replied softly, "all big and white. Can you eat one?"

"So tough you'd like to choke to death."

We were halfway across the river when Edmonia went to the car to get a ginger ale. When she came back she said hesitantly: "Mama, Shadrach has made a fantastic mess in his pants."

"Oh, Lord," said Trixie.

Mr. Dabney clutched the rail and raised his small, pinched, tormented face to heaven. "Ninety-nine years old! Christ almighty! He ain't nothin' but a ninety-nine-years-old *baby*!"

"It smells just awful," said Edmonia.

"Why in the goddamned hell didn't he go to the bathroom before we left?" Mr. Dabney said. "Ain't it bad enough we got to drive three hours to the Farm without——"

"Shoosh!" Trixie interrupted, moving ponderously to the car. "Poor ol' thing, he can't help it. Vernon, you see how you manage your bowels fifty years from now."

Once off the ferry we children giggled and squirmed in the backseat, pointedly squeezed our noses, and scuffled amid the oily rubbish of the floorboards. It *was* an awful smell. But a few miles up the road in the hamlet of Gloucester Court House, drowsing in eighteenth-century brick and ivy, Trixie brought relief to the situation by bidding Mr. Dabney to stop at an Amoco station. Shadrach had partly awakened from his slumbrous trance. He stirred restlessly in his pool of discomfort, and began to make little fretful sounds, so softly restrained as to barely give voice to what must have been his real and terrible distress. "There now, Shad," Trixie said gently, "Trixie'll look after you." And this she did, half-coaxing, half-hoisting the old man from the car and into a standing position, then with the help of Mr. Dabney propelling his skinny scarecrow frame in a suspended tiptoe dance to the rest room marked COLORED, where to the muffled sound of rushing water she performed some careful rite of cleansing and diapering. Then they brought him back to the car. For the first time that morning Shadrach seemed really aroused from that stupor into which he had plunged so swiftly hours before. "Praise de Lawd!" we heard him say, feebly but with spirit, as the elder Dabneys maneuvered him back onto the seat, purified. He gazed about him with glints of recognition, responding with soft chuckles to our little pats of attention. Even Mr. Dabney seemed in sudden good humor. "You comin' along all right now, Shad?" he howled over the rackety clattering sound of the motor. Shadrach nodded and grinned but remained silent. There was a mood in the car of joy and revival. "Slow down, Shoog," Trixie murmured indolently, gulping at a beer, "there might be a speed cop." I was filled with elation, and hope tugged at my heart as the flowering landscape rushed by, green and lush with summer and smelling of hay and honeysuckle.

The Dabney country retreat, as I have said, was dilapidated and rudimentary, a true downfall from bygone majesty. Where there once stood a plantation house of the Palladian stateliness required of its kind during the Tidewater dominion in its heyday, there now roosted a dwelling considerably grander than a shack yet modest by any reckoning. Boxlike, paintless, supported by naked concrete blocks, and crowned by a roof of glistening sheet metal, it would have been an eyesore almost anywhere except in King and Queen County, a bailiwick so distant and underpopulated that the house was scarcely ever viewed by human eyes. A tilted privy out back lent another homely note; junk littered the yard here too. But the soft green acres that surrounded the place were Elysian; the ancient fields and the wild woods rampant with sweet gum and oak and redbud had reverted to the primeval glory of the time of Poca-

hontas and Powhatan. Grapevines crowded the emer-
ald-green thickets that bordered the house on every
side, a delicious winey smell of cedar filled the air, and
the forest at night echoed with the sound of whippoor-
wills. The house itself was relatively clean, thanks not
to any effort on the part of the Dabneys but to the fact
that it remained unlived in by Dabneys for most of the
year.

That day after our fried chicken meal we placed
Shadrach between clean sheets on a bed in one of the
sparsely furnished rooms, then turned to our various
recreations. Little Mole and I played marbles all afternoon just outside the house, seeking the shade of a
majestic old beech tree; after an hour of crawling in the
dirt our faces were streaked and filthy. Later we took a
plunge in the millpond, which, among other things,
purged Little Mole of his B.O. The other children went
fishing for perch and bream in the brackish creek that
ran through the woods. Mr. Dabney drove off to get
provisions at the crossroads store, then vanished into the
underbrush to tinker around his well-hidden still.
Meanwhile Trixie tramped about with heavy footfalls
in the kitchen and downed half a dozen Blue Ribbons,
pausing occasionally to look in on Shadrach. Little Mole
and I peered in, too, from time to time. Shadrach lay in
a deep sleep and seemed to be at peace, even though
now and then his breath came in a ragged gasp and his
long black fingers plucked convulsively at the hem of
the sheet, which covered him to his breast like a white

shroud. Then the afternoon was over. After a dinner of fried perch and bream we all went to bed with the setting of the sun. Little Mole and I lay sprawled naked in the heat on the same mattress, separated by a paper-thin wall from Shadrach's breathing, which rose and fell in my ears against the other night sounds of this faraway and time-haunted place: katydids and crickets and hoot owls and the reassuring cheer—now near, now almost lost—of a whippoorwill.

Late the next morning the county sheriff paid a visit on Mr. Dabney. We were not at the house when he arrived, and so he had to wait for us; we were at the graveyard. Shadrach still slept, with the children standing watch by turns. After our watch Little Mole and I had spent an hour exploring the woods and swinging on the grapevines, and when we emerged from a grove of pine trees a quarter of a mile or so behind the house, we came upon Mr. Dabney and Trixie. They were poking about in a bramble-filled plot of land which was the old Dabney family burial ground. It was a sunny, peaceful place, where grasshoppers skittered in the tall grass. Choked with briars and nettles and weeds and littered with tumbledown stone markers, unfenced and untended for countless decades, it had been abandoned to the encroachments of summer after summer like this one, when even granite and marble had to give way against the stranglehold of spreading roots and voracious green growing things.

All of Mr. Dabney's remote ancestors lay buried here,

together with their slaves, who slept in a plot several feet off to the side—inseparable from their masters and mistresses, but steadfastly apart in death as in life. Mr. Dabney stood amid the tombstones of the slaves, glaring gloomily down at the tangle of vegetation and at the crumbling lopsided little markers. He held a shovel in his hand but had not begun to dig. I peered at the headstones, read the given names, which were as matter-of-fact in their lack of patronymic as the names of spaniels or cats: *Fauntleroy, Wakefield, Sweet Betty, Mary, Jupiter, Lulu. Requiescat in Pace. Anno Domini 1790... 1814... 1831.* All of these Dabneys, I thought, like Shadrach.

"I'll be goddamned if I believe there's a square inch of space left," Mr. Dabney observed to Trixie, and spat a russet gob of tobacco juice into the weeds. "They just crowded all the old dead uncles and mammies they could into this piece of land here. They must be shoulder to shoulder down there." He paused and made his characteristic sound of anguish—a choked dirgelike groan. "Christ Almighty! I hate to think of diggin' about half a ton of dirt!"

"Shoog, why don't you leave off diggin' until this evenin'?" Trixie said. She was trying to fan herself with a soggy handkerchief, and her face—which I had witnessed before in this state of drastic summer discomfort—wore the washed-out bluish shade of skim milk. It usually preceded a fainting spell. "This sun would kill a mule."

Mr. Dabney agreed, saying that he looked forward to a cool glass of iced tea, and we made our way back to the house along a little path of bare earth that wound through a field glistening with goldenrod. Then, just as we arrived at the back of the house we saw the sheriff waiting. He was standing with a foot on the running board of his Plymouth sedan; perched on its front fender was a hulkingly round, intimidating silver siren (in those days pronounced si-*reen*). He was a potbellied middle-aged man with a sun-scorched face fissured with delicate seams, and he wore steel-rimmed spectacles. A gold-plated star was pinned to his civilian shirt, which was soaked with sweat. He appeared hearty, made an informal salute and said: "Mornin', Trixie. Mornin', Vern."

"Mornin', Tazewell," Mr. Dabney replied solemnly, though with an edge of suspicion. Without pause he continued to trudge toward the house. "You want some ice tea?"

"No, thank you," he said. "Vern, hold on a minute. I'd like a word with you."

I was knowledgeable enough to fear in a vague way some involvement with the distillery in the woods, and I held my breath, but then Mr. Dabney halted, turned, and said evenly: "What's wrong?"

"Vern," the sheriff said, "I hear you're fixin' to bury an elderly colored man on your property here. Joe Thornton down at the store said you told him that yesterday. Is that right?"

Mr. Dabney put his hands on his hips and glowered at the sheriff. Then he said: "Joe Thornton is a god-damned incurable blabbermouth. But that's right. What's wrong with that?"

"You can't," said the sheriff.

There was a pause. "Why not?" said Mr. Dabney.

"Because it's against the law."

I had seen rage, especially in matters involving the law, build up within Mr. Dabney in the past. A pulsing vein always appeared near his temple, along with a rising flush in cheeks and brow; both came now, the little vein began to wiggle and squirm like a worm. "What do you mean, it's against the law?"

"Just that. It's against the law to bury anybody on private property."

"*Why* is it against the law?" Mr. Dabney demanded.

"I don't *know* why, Vern," said the sheriff, with a touch of exasperation. "It just *is*, that's all."

Mr. Dabney flung his arm out—up and then down in a stiff, adamant, unrelenting gesture, like a railroad semaphore.

"Down in that field, Tazewell, there have been people buried for nearabout two hundred years. I got an old senile man on my hands. He was a slave and he was born on this place. Now he's dyin' and I've got to bury him here. And I am."

"Vern, let me tell you something," the sheriff said with an attempt at patience. "You will not be permitted to do any such a thing, so please don't try to give me this argument. He will have to be buried in a place where it's legally permitted, like any of the colored church-yards around here, and he will have to be attended to by a licensed colored undertaker. That's the *law*, Commonwealth of Virginia, and there ain't any which, whys, or wherefores about it."

Trixie began to anticipate Mr. Dabney's fury and resentment even before he erupted. "Shoog, keep yourself calm——"

"*Bat shit!* It is an *outrage!*" he roared. "Since when did a taxpaying citizen have to answer to the gov'ment in order to bury a harmless sick old colored man on his own property! It goes against every bill of rights I ever heard of——"

"Shoog!" Trixie put in. "*Please——*" She began to wail.

The sheriff put out placating hands and loudly commanded: "*Quiet!*" Then when Mr. Dabney and Trixie fell silent he went on: "Vern, me an' you have been acquainted for a long time, so please don't give me no trouble. I'm tellin' you for the last time, this. Namely, you have *got* to arrange to get that old man buried at one of the colored churches around here, and you will also have to have him taken care of by a licensed undertaker. You can have your choice. There's a well-known colored undertaker in Tappahannock and also I heard of one over in Middlesex, somewhere near Urbanna or Saluda. If you want, I'll give them a telephone call from the courthouse."

I watched as the red rage in Mr. Dabney's face was

overtaken by a paler, softer hue of resignation. After a brooding long silence, he said: "All right then. *All right!* How much you reckon it'll cost?"

"I don't know exactly, Vern, but there was an old washerwoman worked for me and Ruby died not long ago, and I heard they buried her for thirty-five dollars."

"Thirty-five dollars!" I heard Mr. Dabney breathe. "Christ have mercy!"

Perhaps it was only his rage that caused him to flee, but all afternoon Mr. Dabney was gone and we did not see him again until that evening. Meanwhile, Shadrach rallied for a time from his deep slumber, so taking us by surprise that we thought he might revive completely. Trixie was shelling peas and sipping beer while she watched Little Mole and me at our marbles game. Suddenly Edmonia, who had been assigned to tend to Shadrach for an hour, came running from the house. "Come here, you all, real quick!" she said in a voice out of breath. "Shadrach's wide awake and talking!" And he was: when we rushed to his side we saw that he had hiked himself up in bed, and his face for the first time in many hours wore an alert and knowing expression, as if he were at least partially aware of his surroundings. He had even regained his appetite. Edmonia had put a daisy in the buttonhole of his shirt, and at some point during his amazing resurrection, she said, he had eaten part of it.

"You should have heard him just now," Edmonia

said, leaning over the bed. "He kept talking about going to the millpond. What do you think he meant?"

"Well, could be he just wants to go see the millpond," Trixie replied. She had brought Shadrach a bottle of RC Cola from the kitchen and now she sat beside him, helping him to drink it through a paper straw. "Shad," she asked in a soft voice, "is that what you want? You want to go see the millpond?"

A look of anticipation and pleasure spread over the black face and possessed those old rheumy eyes. And his voice was high-pitched but strong when he turned his head to Trixie and said: "Yes, ma'am, I does. I wants to see de millpond."

"How come you want to see the millpond?" Trixie said gently.

Shadrach offered no explanation, merely said again: "I wants to see de millpond."

And so, in obedience to a wish whose reason we were unable to plumb but could not help honoring, we took Shadrach to see the millpond. It lay in the woods several hundred yards to the east of the house—an ageless murky dammed-up pool bordered on one side by a glade of moss and fern, spectacularly green, and surrounded on all its other sides by towering oaks and elms. Fed by springs and by the same swiftly rushing stream in which the other children had gone fishing, its water mirrored the overhanging trees and the changing sky and was a pleasurable ordeal to swim in, possessing the icy cold that shocks a body to its bones. For a while we could not figure out how to transport Shadrach down to the place; it plainly would not do to let him try to hobble that long distance, propelled, with our clumsy help, on his nearly strengthless legs in their dangling gait. Finally someone thought of the wheelbarrow, which Mr. Dabney used to haul corn to the still. It was fetched from its shed, and we quickly made of it a not unhandsome and passably comfortable sort of a wheeled litter, filling it with hay and placing a blanket on top.

On this mound Shadrach rested easily, with a look of composure, as we moved him gently rocking down the path. I watched him on the way: in my memory he still appears to be a half-blind but self-possessed and serene African potentate being borne in the fullness of his many years to some longed-for, inevitable reward.

We set the wheelbarrow down on the mossy bank, and there for a long time Shadrach gazed at the mill-pond, alive with its skating waterbugs and trembling beneath a copper-colored haze of sunlight where small dragonflies swooped in nervous filmy iridescence. Standing next to the wheelbarrow, out of which the shanks of Shadrach's skinny legs protruded like fragile black reeds, I turned and stared into the ancient face, trying to determine what it was he beheld now that created such a look of wistfulness and repose. His eyes began to follow the Dabney children, who had stripped to their underdrawers and had plunged into the water.

That seemed to be an answer, and in a bright gleam I was certain that Shadrach had once swum here too, during some unimaginable August nearly a hundred years before.

I had no way of knowing that if his long and solitary journey from the Deep South had been a quest to find this millpond and for a recaptured glimpse of childhood, it might just as readily have been a final turning of his back on a life of suffering. Even now I cannot say for certain, but I have always had to assume that the still-young Shadrach who was emancipated in Alabama those many years ago was set loose, like most of his brothers and sisters, into another slavery perhaps more excruciating than the sanctioned bondage. The chronicle has already been a thousand times told of those people liberated into their new and incomprehensible nightmare: of their poverty and hunger and humiliation, of the crosses burning in the night, the random butchery, and, above all, the unending dread. None of that madness and mayhem belongs in this story, but without at least a reminder of these things I would not be faithful to Shadrach. Despite the immense cheerfulness with which he had spoken to us of being "dibested of mah plenty," he must have endured unutterable adversity. Yet his return to Virginia, I can now see, was out of no longing for the former bondage, but to find an earlier innocence. And as a small boy at the edge of the millpond I saw Shadrach not as one who had fled darkness, but as one who had searched for light refracted within a flashing moment of remembered childhood. As Shadrach's old clouded eyes gazed at the millpond with its plunging and calling children, his face was suffused with an immeasurable calm and sweetness, and I sensed that he had recaptured perhaps the one pure, untroubled moment in his life. "Shad, did you go swimming here too?" I said. But there was no answer. And it was not long before he was drowsing again; his head fell to the side and we rolled him back to the house in the wheelbarrow.

On Saturday nights in the country the Dabneys usually went to bed as late as ten o'clock. That evening Mr. Dabney returned at suppertime, still sullen and fretful but saying little, still plainly distraught and sick over the sheriff's mandate. He did not himself even pick up a fork. But the supper was one of those ample and blessed meals of Trixie's I recall so well. Only the bounty of a place like the Tidewater backcountry could provide such a feast for poor people in those hardpressed years: ham with red-eye gravy, grits, collard greens, okra, sweet corn, huge red tomatoes oozing juice in a salad with onions and herbs and vinegar. For dessert there was a delectable bread pudding drowned in fresh cream. Afterward, a farmer and bootlegging colleague from down the road named Mr. Seddon R. Washington arrived in a broken-down pickup truck to join with Mr. Dabney at the only pastime I ever saw him engage in—a game of dominoes. Twilight fell and the oil lanterns were lit. Little Mole and I went back like dull slugs to our obsessive sport, scratching a large circle in the dust beside the porch and crouching down with our crystals and agates in a moth-crazed oblong of lantern light, tiger-yellow and flickering. A full moon rose slowly out of the edge of the woods like an immense, bright, faintly smudged balloon. The clicking of our marbles alternated with the click-click of the dominoes on the porch bench.

"If you wish to know the plain and simple truth about whose fault it is," I heard Mr. Dabney explain to Mr. Washington, "you can say it is the fault of your Franklin D-for-Disaster Roosevelt. The Dutchman millionaire. And his so-called New Deal ain't worth diddley squat. You know how much I made last year—legal, that is?"

"How much?" said Mr. Washington.

"I can't even tell you. It would shame me. They are colored people sellin' deviled crabs for five cents apiece on the streets in Newport News made more than me. There is an injustice somewhere with this system." He paused. "Eleanor's near about as bad as he is." Another pause. "They say she fools around with colored men and Jews. Preachers mainly."

"Things bound to get better," Mr. Washington said.

"They can't get no worse," said Mr. Dabney. "I can't get a job anywhere. I'm unqualified. I'm only qualified for making whiskey."

Footsteps made a soft slow padding sound across the

porch and I looked up and saw Edmonia draw near her father. She parted her lips, hesitated for a moment, then said: "Daddy, I think Shadrach has passed away."

Mr. Dabney said nothing, attending to the dominoes with his expression of pinched, absorbed desperation and muffled wrath. Edmonia put her hand lightly on his shoulder. "Daddy, did you hear what I said?"

"I heard."

"I was sitting next to him, holding his hand, and then all of a sudden his head—it just sort of rolled over and he was still and not breathing. And his hand—it just got limp and—well, what I mean, cold." She paused again. "He never made a sound."

Mr. Washington rose with a cough and walked to the far edge of the porch, where he lit a pipe and gazed up at the blazing moon. When again Mr. Dabney made no response, Edmonia lightly stroked the edge of his shoulder and said gently: "Daddy, I'm afraid."

"What're you afraid about?" he replied.

"I don't know," she said with a tremor. "Dying. It scares me. I don't know what it means—death. I never saw anyone—like that before."

"Death ain't nothin' to be afraid about," he blurted in a quick, choked voice. "It's life that's fearsome! *Life!*" Suddenly he arose from the bench, scattering dominoes to the floor, and when he roared "*Life!*" again, I saw Trixie emerge from the black hollow of the front door and approach with footfalls that sent a shudder through the porch timbers. "Now, *Shoog*—" she began.

"*Life* is where you've got to be terrified!" he cried as the unplugged rage spilled forth. "Sometimes I understand why men commit suicide! Where in the goddamned hell am I goin' to get the money to put him in the ground? Niggers have always been the biggest problem! Goddamnit, I was brought up to have a certain respect and say 'colored' instead of 'niggers' but they are always a problem. They will always just drag you down! I ain't got thirty-five-dollars! I ain't got *twenty-five* dollars! I ain't got *five* dollars!"

"*Vernon!*" Trixie's voice rose, and she entreatingly spread out her great creamy arms. "Someday you're goin' to get a *stroke!*"

"And one other thing!" He stopped.

Then suddenly his fury——or the harsher, wilder part of it——seemed to evaporate, sucked up into the moonlit night with its soft summery cricketing sounds and its scent of warm loam and honeysuckle. For an instant he looked shrunken, runtier than ever, so light and frail that he might blow away like a leaf, and he ran a nervous, trembling hand through his shock of tangled black hair. "I know, I know," he said in a faint, unsteady voice edged with grief. "Poor old man, he couldn't help it. He was a decent, pitiful old thing, probably never done anybody the slightest harm. I ain't got a thing in the world against Shadrach. Poor old man."

Crouching below the porch I felt an abrupt, smothering misery. The tenderest gust of wind blew from the woods and I shivered at its touch on my cheek, mourn-

ing for Shadrach and Mr. Dabney, and slavery and
destitution, and all the human discord swirling around
me in a time and place I could not understand. As if to
banish my fierce unease, I began to try—in a seizure of
concentration—to count the fireflies sparkling in the
night air. Eighteen, nineteen, twenty . . .

"And anyway," Trixie said, touching her husband's
hand, "he died on Dabney ground like he wanted to.
Even if he's got to be put away in a strange graveyard."

"Well, he won't know the difference," said Mr. Dabney. "When you're dead nobody knows the difference.
Death ain't much."

A
Tidewater
Morning

During the late summer of 1938, there was black news of the onrushing war. I had just turned thirteen, and I had a newspaper route that carried me on foot up and down the hot, sycamore-lined streets of our little village on the banks of the James River in Tidewater Virginia. I folded the papers into cylinders, forty-five or fifty of them, and stuffed them into a dingy white canvas bag that I lugged around with a strap that at first cut painfully into my shoulder, then eased up about a third of the way through my afternoon trek, which took about an hour and a half. The banner headlines that summer were tall and thick with harsh alarm: HITLER THREATENS. GERMAN TROOPS MASSING. CZECHOSLOVAKIA MENACED. The news caused me less fear, really, than a vague, visceral excitement, distracting me from the gloom that encompassed me, from the ache that swelled in my stomach whenever I thought of my mother and her illness. And that thought always returned with a queasy jolt. I was also nagged by a worry having to do with my body: my nipples had become exquisitely tender, sensitive to the touch of the inside of my shirt and to my nervous, examining fingers, and the horrible fantasy flashed off and on in my mind that I might be turning, at least partially, into a girl. I fretted over other matters—over the length and tedium of the paper route, which I had commenced in the jazzed-up high spirits of anyone at his first paid professional employment but which had now lost most of its savor, and over my pay: $2.50 a week for nine hours, including an extra tour of duty overloaded at dawn with the fat editions of Sunday. Even during the Depression this was paltry recompense, and it was doled out dime by dime, nickel by nickel, by the only consummately mean-spirited person among the many frail and imperfect characters who floated in and out of my early youth.

Mr. Quigley—I have forgotten or blanked out his first name—was the proprietor of Quigley's Store, an all-purpose emporium that stood on a barren tract of land just east of the village. It was a squat, nondescript place made of brick painted a bleached blue with a squeaking screen door and two windows nearly opaque with dust where one neon sign, reading PABST BLUE RIBBON, pulsed spiritlessly, and the other, reading SCHLITZ, was permanently dark. I imagine that if one could smell a Hogarth drawing, it would smell of gin; the interior of Quigley's Store, Hogarthian in its dim clutter and squalor, smelled of spilled beer, cigarette smoke, and unwashed floors. After four o'clock a flock of shipyard workers gathered there every weekday afternoon to knock down bottles of beer at the round metal-topped tables in the rear of the store; they were a sullen lot, mostly displaced North Carolinians who had come to the area to make a few desperately needed shipyard dollars, and they lolled around in near-silence in the murk, chewing on pickled pigs' feet from a rotund two-gallon jar and munching on pretzels. Up front was a magazine stand with its ranks of comic books, *True Detectives*, and *Police Gazettes*. Next to this sat a grimy soda fountain, seldom used, and a display case of candy bars where I could always see the half-dozen resident flies making their perpendicular strolls on the glass inside. There were two pinball machines whose *bunk bong ding, ding bunk bong* was a constant background monotone. After the five miles of my paper route I was invariably sweat-soaked and nearly faint with thirst. So, together with the two or three other boys straggling in, I would head straight for the red enamel storage chest where, alongside the beer, the Coca-Colas were kept, and the Nehi and the Orange Crush and the Hires root beer. No stately automated dispensers in those days, no color-coordinated seven-foot-tall designer model popping out its temperature-regulated frosted can into the dry and welcoming palm. One went instead to the case where the bottles stood in water cooled by ice, withdrew a Coca-Cola or a Dr Pepper refreshingly damp between one's fingers. In all civilized establishments the water was changed regularly; at Quigley's the water stagnated week in and week out, and the malodorous bottle, withdrawn, was slimy to the touch. Whenever I would hurry to the case and open the top, Mr. Quigley would be waiting with his smudged and tattered notebook, pencil poised.

"What are you having, Whitehurst?" he would ask.

In those stuffier times businessmen were often on a last-name basis with their employees, but though I was a boy, it would have taken someone less rigidly uncharitable than Mr. Quigley to call me Paul. I hated the stingy bastard.

"I'm having a root beer," I would reply.

And I'd watch him as he'd scratch my name in his notebook, or indite some intricate cross-reference or computation, and dock me five cents. Mr. Quigley's ethnicity was somewhat odd for a native Virginian; it was said that his mother was Greek. He was a swarthy, pinched-face little man with a pronounced curvature of the spine that twisted him slightly sideways and gave him a limp. Was it this handicap, producing some inner misery of spirit—I occasionally wondered later (having become less uncharitable myself)—that disposed him to his lack of generosity? I was not so impractical or dumb about finance, especially at that time, when a dollar was worth a dollar, to begrudge Mr. Quigley his concern about the attrition that many unaccounted-for Coca-Colas or Hershey bars would produce against his profits. I did resent, though, the absence in him of any hint of humor or benevolence—for I was still enough of a child to expect the preferential decency, at least, that a child is *supposed* to receive—and I resented most of all that never once (*never once, never once,* I would mutter to myself as I slogged across the lawns deep in garden-hose damp and dog shit) did he offer me a small treat, gratis. Not a candy bar, not a bag of potato chips, nor even the pack of peanut butter crackers ("Nibble a NAB for a Nickel") I would snatch off its filthy shelf when, some Friday evening, my stomach growled with unpropitiated hunger. He would be waiting. Down would go Mr. Quigley's pencil in his notebook, marking my tiny debit, and as I glanced up at the pinched, small, satisfied face I made a rapid calculation and realized that on this payday I'd take home less than half my salary, or around $1.15.

There were a couple of Quigley offspring, a boy and a girl, but I had never seen them; they were considerably older than I and had already dropped out of high school. But nearly always present was Mrs. Quigley, a tough old graying slattern who chain-smoked corktipped Raleigh cigarettes and slapped around in bedroom slippers with red feather pompons as she served beer and pigs' feet and tried to cheer up the disconsolate rednecks. Sometimes she wore hair curlers all day long. Her jokes were dirty and they made me cringe a little, while I listened with one ear and folded my newspapers. I wasn't really a prude, since I had recently passed from the relative purity of grammar school into high school, where the common lingo swarmed with obscenities. Yet Mrs. Quigley was almost the first adult and certainly the only woman I knew out of whose mouth flowed, with the liquid ease of ordinary discourse, a stream of four-letter words. "Hey, Brighteyes," she'd say to one of the sadder beer guzzlers, "let go of your dick and have another Schlitz." I was torn between shock and enchantment, but often my giggles prevailed, since her slovenly good cheer was an antidote to her husband's ill nature; more than once she slipped me a Mounds bar or a tepid ginger ale. In the end she was the only colorful spot in these dismal afternoons and Sunday mornings, and I may even have developed, before my labors ended, a distant crush, finding irresistible the way she belched, loud and with blowsy relish, or the moment when she raised her rayon shift and displayed to the gaping Carolinians a heavy blue-veined thigh tattooed with a fading red poinsettia.

Then there was Ralph, the store drudge. He pushed boxes around and did the heavy lifting in the back room and cleaned up the tables after the customers left. Ralph worked long hours, but I figured he was paid not much more than our newsboys' coolie wages. Whatever he was paid, Mr. Quigley prized him for the sport he provided, this dim-witted Negro, ginger-colored and freckled, pear-shaped with a slue-footed waddle and a high, fluting voice like a castrato's. His trouble was, I suspect, glandular, but Mr. Quigley exploited it as a sideshow attraction for the group gathered around the steel-topped tables; Ralph complied, in fact cooperated, as many a black man—some much brighter than Ralph—did in that era, when it was smarter to be Stepin Fetchit or Rochester than a smartass. "Ralph," he would say, "did you know that you are about the weirdest-goddamned-sounding Knee-grow there is?" "Yassah," Ralph would pipe. Then, hurt: "Nawsuh."

Then "Yassah" again, with a grin frozen in a desire to please. "You sound like a goddamned dickeybird." "Yassah." "Or a tree toad." "Yassah." I lived in a racist society and had been inoculated so early against the idea of equality that a part of me supinely went along with the prevailing view that Negroes were a lesser breed of human being. But parental enlightenment and my own conscience—I would like to think it was no more complicated than Huck Finn's—caused me to know otherwise. My skin crawled at Mr. Quigley's loutish treatment of Ralph; it troubled me only slightly more than Ralph's tame, grinning submission. "Ralph," he would announce in an aside to the customers, "is the world's goosiest burrhead." A low hum from the group, and a single cackle. "I'm gone show you all something truly amazing." The routine was set up, craftily prepared, Ralph feigning unconcern as he swabbed at a table, the fat behind in baggy trousers presenting itself amid the smoke, swaying. Mr. Quigley (this *grown man*, I would think while I watched) would sneak up on Ralph through the crowd, his pinched dark face creased with delight, anticipating. And then the sudden pounce, the goose in the rear, and Ralph, floundering upward with clumsy, exaggerated panic, arms flailing, the voice a falsetto wail. "Oh, Lawd, Lawd, ooooeeee!" Howls from the crowd, thumping bottles, general pleasure and gratitude. And Ralph would waddle around a bit, beaming in the shower of applause, and lick his lips in absurd self-approval. After these performances, sometimes Mr.

Quigley would give Ralph a soft drink or a candy bar, which, I always reflected, was more than he ever gave me. I'd hoist my bag to my shoulder and head out into the clammy heat, thinking, *The dumb black son of a bitch, how can he take that?* Then the fact of the misfortune of his color would crowd in on me, and my contempt for Ralph would be replaced by my loathing for Mr. Quigley and his grossness, his niggardly heart.

In the early morning hours of a September Sunday, I lay in bed listening to the sounds of my mother's suffering. It was a few days before her fifty-first birthday. For the eight years she had endured the cancer the pain had sometimes been severe, but it had usually been of the sort that with immense struggle she could bear; now in these final weeks her strength had drained away. Creeping through her bones, the pain had become insistent, nearly without letup. I awoke at about one, aroused by her quavering cry in the front room. Then the tiptoeing feet of the nurse, Miss Slocum, followed by the heavier footsteps of my father. In my mother's room Miss Slocum made soft, sibilant sounds, indistinct; my father's voice, a tone louder, began to come intermittently in words that were distraught and tortured. That evening an announcement on the radio downstairs had spoken of a heat wave, a record for the season; I lay soaked in sweat beneath a black electric fan, which in each half-circle of its rotation allowed the heat to engulf me, then cooled me with a puny puff of air. From the dense darkness outside my window, where, I knew, fireflies winked among my mother's two small flower beds, I inhaled a sugary odor of late-blooming clematis. Other Septembers the white cascading vine had smelled delicious; now in the night it made me feel a little sick. Again I heard Miss Slocum's whispery syllables of comfort, touched with strain.

Suddenly my mother screamed——a scream, long and hopeless, containing a note of anguish like nothing I had ever heard before. It was a shriek that swept up and down my naked body like a flame. It was an alien sound, which is to say unexpectedly beyond my sense of logic and my experience, so that for the barest instant it had the effect of something histrionic, out of the movies, a Frankenstein-Dracula film in which a bad actress emoted implausible terror. But it was real, and I plunged my face into my pillow, wrapping it about my head like a humid caul. I tried to shut out the scream. Deaf, in darkness, I sought to think of anything but that scream. I thought of Miss Slocum, who was a buxom woman of about thirty with an open, dimpled, heartlike face scrubbed mirror-bright; she resembled a fattened earthbound Sonja Henie and possessed an arresting defect: vestigial thumbs that were attached to the outside of her normal thumbs. This is a grotesquerie that I almost wish I didn't have to record. But it is an actual part of a complex remembrance. There had been a touch of dark mirth in my mother's desire, six months before, to fire Miss Slocum as soon as she had been hired, when the extra thumbs were suddenly perceived; becoming daily more helpless, my mother required bathing and massage, and she had professed abhorrence at the idea of twelve digits stroking her flesh. Why, in God's name, she asked my father, hadn't she had them removed? She was especially repelled when she noticed that Miss Slocum kept the little thumbs manicured, but I heard my father explain that this was not unreasonable, really; wouldn't neglected thumbs be more attention-getting, and so forth. Anyway, the matter was resolved—besides, the nurse was a treasure, utterly patient and gentle. When I unwrapped my head from the pillow, the screaming had stopped.

"Miss Slocum, you *must* give her more morphine," I heard my father's voice, hoarse, nearer, outside my door.

"I cain't, Mr. Whitehurst, I just cain't," came the reply. She spoke in the accents of the Virginia hill country, a throaty, soft treble from the steep slopes and hollow, which, although I never really knew or asked about her upbringing, always made me think of an amiably disheveled *Li'l Abner* family—half a dozen towheaded brothers and sisters, a moonshiner father, a mother whose lip bulged with a tuck of snuff. I had become fond of her simple, countrified tenderness, the artless compassion that she lavished on my mother day after hot summer day, bathing her, changing her, trying to soothe her remediless misery. "I just cain't give her any more morphine. Dr. Beecroft won't allow it. He gave me instructions. I cain't give her any more just now."

"You *must* give her more. I can't stand what she's having to bear."

"I cain't, Mr. Whitehurst," she insisted patiently. "You must understand that. Please believe me. There is a certain dose—there is—and you mustn't go beyond that."

"It's past endurance, that pain!" His voice rose, at the edge of breaking. "She's going mad!"

"Dr. Beecroft will be here soon, Mr. Whitehurst," she replied. "You must please talk to him. I'm sure he's going to do what he can." I heard their footsteps as they moved back toward my mother's bedroom.

In the half-light my eyes roamed around my room, a cramped space, the room of an only child, tidy, organized, with the possessory feel of everything in place, unmolested by any of the brothers and sisters I had for years longed to have and now, in my desolation, longed for with a special ache. The village had many children. It was a place and an era of busy procreation. The houses of the village, small-scale as they appeared, were swollen with vigorous, rowdy families, and my friends all had siblings I envied for the very fact of their being—splendid older brothers, sensible younger sisters; even the little runny-nosed brats at the bottom of the family chain I would have loved to cuddle and protect. Once when a neighbor daughter was killed in a horse-riding fall, I saw the overspilling fountain of love and solace that welled up from the heart of the family, brothers and sisters embracing and hugging, clinging to each other, as if their grief were lessened by simple contact with their common origin of flesh. And for some nights they slept sprawled together in one big bed, holding on to one another, preventing even sleep from separating them in their mourning. In my room I felt as alone as if I were in a dungeon. The heat was malign, smothering, and I gasped like a fish in the darkness. The crack from the door sent a wedge of light against the wall above me with its heroic frieze: the Fordham backfield in Kodachrome. And the edge of my bookshelf, the light bisecting *Mr. Midshipman Easy*, *The Swiss Family Robinson*, *Les Misérables*, *Ferdinand*, volumes one through four of *The Book of Knowledge*. "Gently, gently," I heard my father say, "oh, please gently, Miss Slocum." And at the light's dimmest reach: FIRST PRIZE, ORAL READING, TIDEWATER REGION, VIRGINIA PUBLIC SCHOOLS. Laurie Macauley had died of a broken neck. No one knew why the mare had bolted; she had been seraphically gentle, a paragon of equine docility. But Laurie and the horse had remained lost in the woods near the C & O tracks for a day and a night, and when they discovered the body, part of her face had been eaten away by vermin, preventing the open-coffin viewing that would have been customary. I squirmed on the wet sheets, thinking: *I don't understand this.*

I felt thirsty—an urgent, serious thirst of the kind

that seized me after my newspaper route. I got up from bed and slipped on my pajama bottom, opened the door just wide enough so that I could slide through, and then slipped downstairs on tiptoeing bare feet so that my father and Miss Slocum wouldn't hear me. The kitchen, like the other rooms of the house, was skimpy and confined; I darted over the ripples of the linoleum floor in three steps, opened the refrigerator, and groped in the dark interior for the jar of ice water. Then I lifted the jar and gulped, my eyes moistening over in appreciation even as I sensed a twitch of guilt. I knew I shouldn't be drinking from the jar. One didn't swap germs promiscuously at a time when common infections sometimes spelled doom. Surfaces were wiped clean, made sterile; raw food was triply rinsed and purified. As people moved through an invisible blizzard of evil microbes, there was much random mortality. Mr. Max Weissberger, owner of the leading department store in the town nearby, scratched a pimple on his nose on a Thursday, and by Monday he was dead. On the main floor at the store, near the perfume counter and on the wall between the elevators, a portrait plaque in bronze memorializing Max Weissberger always caught my glance, which was then drawn inevitably to the tip of the burnished nose and its pathetic vulnerability. It could be a scary world, pre-penicillin, but I thought some of those like my mother were overly zealous: the memory of the moment when, still ambulant and sharp-eyed, she let me have it for drinking from the jar was bright in my mind as I gulped away. And my guilt was intensified by everything that was going on upstairs. I replaced the jar in the refrigerator and turned to see the glow from the alcove just off the kitchen, where there was situated a single cot and a lamp. In that alcove, smaller than a jail cell, there was also a cheap tabletop radio so battered and overused that the inner wiring poked out of the Bakelite case; it was playing now but turned down very low, low enough so that I hadn't heard it until this moment, when I approached, and knew whom I would see sitting there on the cot, listening, just as I knew exactly—or almost exactly—what she would be listening to. I had heard it with Florence a dozen times before. The blurred murmur grew louder, more distinct, defining itself as a voice sweetly insinuating at first but then swelling into wild, strident exhortation: *"Be it known therefore unto you that the salvation of God is sent unto the Gentiles, and they will HEAR it!"* A massed congregational response: *"Amen! Yes! Amen!"* The sound was that of some prophet whooping and hollering through remote nocturnal distances—50,000 watts vaulting the Appalachians from Cincinnati or Detroit or Pittsburgh: a jam-packed tabernacle, a choir of white-robed angels, a sweating black divine reaching out to believers across the miles of ether. Florence, squatting on the edge of the cot, looked up startled when I appeared, and said, "Sonny, sonny. Paul, baby, you should be asleep." *"Heal dem, Jesus, HEAL dem!"* She switched the radio off.

Throughout the last several years Florence had spent the night in the alcove—as she was doing now—whenever my father had to be away, a rare happening, or during some bad turn in the steadily declining health of Miss Adelaide, as she called my mother. Ordinarily, if I was up this late, I would sit and listen with Florence to these evangelical jamborees. I loved them, although I would never have admitted this to my friends. I loved them mainly for the music. The hysteric preaching was beyond my grasp, but the singing stirred my blood, thrilled me, aroused in me a latent sense of Christian joy and glory long stilled by "Abide with Me" and other such whiney Presbyterian solicitations. When the far-off choirs burst into gospel hymns like "Precious Jesus" and "Didn't It Rain!" I got a charge that began to encircle my bottom and then moved straight up my spine to my skull, where it climaxed in a mini-electro-cution, setting all the hairs of my scalp on end. Most of the time Florence and I would listen together, she nodding and mouthing the words, and she'd squeeze her eyes shut and press her bony brown hand into mine. But tonight there was silence after she turned the radio off. I sat down beside her, hearing the hum of the refrigerator and the shrilling of the katydids in the sycamore trees.

I saw her roll her eyes toward the room upstairs. There was something hesitant in that glance, hesitant and fearful, as if she were anticipating once more a repetition of the scream that had sent me diving into my pillow. Then her eyes softened and she said to me: "We done had some happy times in dis yere house. Sad times but happy times too. You got to remember de happy times, baby." She paused. "You gettin' so old I got to stop callin' you baby."

"When was a happy time, Flo?" I said.

"Well, day was yo' birthday 'bout three years ago, before yo' mother fell down and broke her leg and had to put on dat brace and all, when we all went to Buckroe Beach—remember, you and Mr. Jeff and Miss Adelaide and 'bout twenty-five yo' friends from school—and I fixed fried chicken and biscuits and all. Remember, we built a fire on the sand and all? And Miss Adelaide was walkin' up and down the beach, singing'. Dat sho was a happy time." I watched her as she spoke, a melancholy, large-nosed brown woman, angular of face and with a stooped, angular body, gazing into space in distant reflection as she stroked absently at her chin. She had worked for us as cook and maid for seven or eight years. Her crankiness had become legendary. She almost never smiled, couldn't crack a smile even when greeting guests—an uncorrectable trait that my mother had tried vainly to correct. Everyone had regarded Florence as "exceedingly competent" or "well trained" but hopelessly sullen. I knew better since I simply knew *her* better, and as a little kid I'd hung for interminable hours around the kitchen, where I learned that her sullenness was in truth a grim, grievous equanimity, the outcome of a daily struggle to keep her composure in the face of unending family catastrophes. Despite her glowering countenance, despite her pay (five dollars a week, plus meals and totin' privileges, standard throughout the village), Florence was unfailingly loyal to our tiny, disintegrating family—patient with my father, who was becoming more and more unstrung as the time passed, and gently protective but strict with me, over whom she had thrown, so naturally that I had scarcely realized its presence, the cloak of surrogate motherhood. And she attended to my mother's needs like some tireless and consecrated priestess. I think she had began to mourn her, in the dark privacy of her already ravaged heart, long before my father and I were really aware of what was happening. "And dat Christmastime two or three years ago," she went on, patting my knee, "when Mr. Harry Bladen was drunk and dat French wife of his got so steamin' mad she po'd a bottle of wine over his head. An' Miss Adelaide she laughed so much she almost choked on the capon I cooked. Dat was a happy time. 'Member that? And we thought you wasn't goin' to get no bicycle on account of the sto' didn't deliver it the day before. But the man from the sto' came on Christmas Day, and there that wheel was just shinin', and you about so happy you just ready to blow away."

I'm going to discharge that woman as soon as she comes, first thing tomorrow morning. I can no longer stand that colored woman around.

Adelaide, I'm telling you, you will do no such thing. She's been with us for four years now and she's hardworking and faithful. Except for once or twice when she was ill she's not missed a single day. Even in that fantastic hurricane she was here, when the trolleys had stopped running!

I can't have her working here anymore. I can't put up with this absolutely hangdog manner! This Yessum and No'm spoken with such hostility, as if I had requested some incredibly arduous service. And when Louise Marable, trying to be nice, trying not to offend, suggests nonetheless, as you heard her tonight, that there is a big difference between polite reserve and rudeness, then I feel it's the last straw. She's out as of tomorrow morning. O-u-t.

Adelaide, let me tell you something. Let me be candid. I think you've come a long, long way in the years since we first knew each other. We've discussed this before, and you will recollect your own admission that you came to Virginia with a load of ugly prejudices about colored people. Such an irony, too, a Pennsylvanian, a college graduate—sophisticated, widely traveled, reader of William Faulkner, bien élevée, *and all that—carrying around this baggage of truly bizarre notions about colored people, as you still prefer to call them, or Negroes, as I call them. Crudely, if I might jog your memory, you said they all smelled—like onions, or perhaps garlic, if recollection serves me right—and you also uttered the howler that in terms of physiognomy there was no way to tell one Negro from another. And I remember clearly when Paul was about five your telling him to say "colored woman," not "lady." Good gracious, the ways of the world are strange. Here I was, not the grandson, mind you, but the son of a slave owner, born in a county 45 percent Negro, and reared in an atmosphere so benighted as regards this one matter that I was a fully grown adult before I realized that despite formal manumission, these people had continued to dwell in a state of slavery, in many ways worse. I don't mean to sound self-righteous but it was I who had to teach you, not you me, that Negroes had essential qualities of dignity and decency. I, a shit-kicking Carolina yokel who, when I first met you, suspected you of being a neo-abolitionist—*

Jefferson, stop, you are missing the point entirely—

Wait a minute, Adelaide, and then you can proceed. I fully concede that your attitudes have changed remarkably in recent years. You have become, if, by my standards, not quite truly open-minded, then certainly tolerant, and your sense of fair play is exemplary when stacked up against that of some of the bigoted friends you play with, and of the other adherents of the dinosaur politics of Harry Byrd with his execrable poll tax and other felonies—

And that is the point, Jefferson! It's not her color, it's her class! She's a servant! She's of the servant class, the class that served our family in Connellsville, some Irish, some German, some Hungarian, but servants! Mama and Daddy asked only that they be pleasant-mannered, and

finally that's all I'm asking of this sullen, evil-spirited
Florence you've supported so long——

That was a few years before, and my mother had, at
last, come around to a frank affection for Florence,
sullen or whatever, smile or no smile. In the alcove
Florence and I sat silently together for a while, listening. We were alert to the motions upstairs, awaiting a
murmur, a voice, even the creaking of a floorboard, but
we heard nothing. And thus the silence, I knew, meant
that my father and Miss Slocum had again taken up
their vigil at my mother's bedside, creating that virtually motionless tableau which——whenever I stole past
the room, forbidden to go in——appeared to have existed
immemorially, like some old painting or illustration I
had seen (or thought I had seen) called "The Sickroom":
the recumbent form in the blue nightgown, unsheeted
in the heat, only the bare, withered calves showing, and
the bruised-looking skeletal feet; the shirt-sleeved back
of my father bent forward in his chair, obscuring my
mother's face, his tense arms seeming to be suspended
in the act of a frantic embrace; Miss Slocum gazing
from the other side of the bed with a look of pensive
dreaminess, unperturbed, the light glinting from the
starched cap resting like a white tiara upon the crest of
her permanent wave. Behind all, the massed flowers——
gladioli, white and yellow roses, tulips, bunched ar-
rangements in wicker baskets with wicker handles. And
an electric fan on a stand sweeping a dread stench from

the room: overripe blossoms and acrid medicine. Florence and I listened, turned to glance at each other, listened again, heard nothing but the katydids shrilling in the darkness. The night was fecund and sweet-smelling with clematis. "You know, Paul," Florence said finally, "I heered tell of many folks got well from what yo' mama got, worse off dan her. Yes, many folks. Dere was dis white lady in Suffolk who was jest as sick as yo' mama. I heered tell of her not long ago. She was a long, long time in bed and sufferin' and takin' mo'phine and all, and suddenly she got well. One night she was layin' there in dis great pain and de peoples was givin' her mo'phine an' all, and she just began to speak and she rose up on her feet and walked. And she was all well. From den on she was well and jest as healthy as you an' me. It was de spirit of God dat saved dat woman. It was de grace of Jesus Christ an' his salvation."

"That would be wonderful," I began. I had for a moment the oddest stir of hope, a flutter in my chest. Then it vanished. "I don't think I believe in all that. I mean the woman getting well—maybe she did. But the salvation part, I really don't think so. I think Jesus is okay, but—" I broke off.

"Den how come you go to church?"

"Well, you know, we don't go to church all that regularly. I haven't been to Sunday school in two or three months, or church either."

"Den how come yo' daddy goes?"

"I've told you all that before, Flo. Papa goes because

of tradition and because he loves the beauty of the Scriptures and the ethical values of Christianity. He once told me that he went and made me go because I might absorb some of the teachings of Christ having to do with justice. Mostly it's for me, I guess."

"Does yo' daddy *believe*, you think, Paul? Believe in de Holy Spirit an' de power of de blood and prayer?"

I hesitated for a long time, then said: "I don't know, Flo. I don't think so. He gets awfully mad at religion sometimes. He says he's a skeptic." After another pause, I went on: "Once Papa told me that whenever there was a long prayer in church he spoke to himself lines from Rilke, who is a German poet."

In the shadows I sensed Florence slowly shaking her head back and forth. "Po-*et* Dat is some sad shame." In a moment she said softly: "I think I'll go upstairs and see how Miss Adelaide is. I ain't goin' to be but a minute. When I gits back I want you to go to bed. Ain't dis Sunday mornin'? Ain't you got yo' paper route?"

"Yes."

"What time?"

"Five o'clock," I replied.

"Je-*sus*, dat's what I thought! Now you got to git to bed right away, you hear me?"

Between the kitchen and the dining room there was another alcove, somewhat larger than the first, which was my mother's music room. Something compelled me to go there, and I went into the room just as I heard Florence's feet climbing the stairs above me. I turned on the gooseneck lamp that rested on the upright piano; the little sanctum was aglow with a soft bronze light that illuminated this place treasured by my mother above all other places in the house, or indeed anywhere; shelf upon shelf of bound sheet music, the walls lower down lined with shellac records in albums whose spines bore titles in bright or fading shades of gold. These she and my father played on a fancy cabinet model Atwater Kent electric phonograph, "superheterodyne," advanced in sound for the day but tending toward fogginess unless the steel needle was changed after a dozen or so discs. There was to me no corny iconolatry in the plaster busts of Schubert, of Beethoven, of Brahms; if they were the saints my mother worshiped, their presence was manifestly justified. Atop the piano there were photographs, framed, inscribed. These she had acquired as others collect pictures of Hollywood divinities. *Für Adelaide*, read one, above chicken scratches in German, signed *Gustav Mahler*, a scholarly-looking man with a pleasant, slightly insane gleam. Another: *To Adelaide Whitehurst, with kindest regards, Ernestine Schumann-Heink*. Arturo Toscanini, fierce. Fritz Kreisler, gemütlich. Lotte Lehmann, fatuously regal. One picture with no inscription save the place and year—Vienna, 1904—always held my gaze, since it showed my young mother herself in a garland of brown braids, with eyeglasses and dressed in a bosomy high-collared blouse and long pleated skirt, smiling a bright-toothed smile that was clearly a smile of sheer infatuation for the whiskered old satyr against whose paunch she leaned—her voice teacher, one Herr "Rudi" Reichardt. It was he who, one sweet and priceless day over thirty years before, had introduced her to Mahler. Squinting down, I saw that the sheet of music on the piano was from Schubert's *Winterreise*. I was still only half-educated, musically speaking. I had not yet really made myself familiar with the songs my mother sang, the seemingly limitless outpouring of *Lieder* by Schubert and Schumann and Brahms and a dozen others that she had let spring forth from that little room, in her lovely, clear contralto, a sound that always seemed to me to possess an actual coloration, opalescent, like pearl. They all flowed in and out of one another, these unfathomable songs; I could name just a few of them. They were linked together only by a voice that gave them a sometimes festive, sometimes somber tenderness. Few people in the village cared for such music or listened to it seriously; even so, no one considered my mother odd or freakish, and in fact once in a while children would gather along the fence of our backyard, along with a few grown-ups, and listen to her, clapping when she finished with mild but real appreciation for these joyous and plaintive tunes, these alien lyrics so far removed from the aesthetic of the *Lucky Strike Program* and Kay Kyser's *Kollege of Musical Knowledge*, Guy Lombardo, and other porridge oozing from the radio. But her music, and therefore her chief pleasure in life, had been dealt a fearful blow a couple of years before. One afternoon she tripped and fell in one of her flower beds. It should have been a harmless tumble but it wasn't; the cancer had begun to riddle her bones, and her leg was broken beyond any hope of mending. And so the brace she was compelled to put on, a gruesome contraption of steel and leather straps that she had to wear when standing or walking, or when she was propped up at a right angle while sitting, kept her thereafter from playing the piano at all. This caused her wicked distress, but it didn't entirely daunt her. She was so indefatigably wed to her songs that often she simply sang without accompaniment; harmony was lost but the fine voice carried on, weakening and fading away only as her body itself was overcome by feebleness and she could walk no more. One of my last memories of her before she became bedridden for good was of her standing in her garden, amid the vivid May blooms and darting hummingbirds and the fidget of bees. Her back was to me, for a while she was motionless, and then she took one or two hobbled steps with her brace and cane. At once, from the way she bowed her head, I knew she was going to sing. There was an indrawn breath, a faltering first note, and I heard her voice rise in clear, untroubled, hymnal melody.

Ist auf deinem Psalter,
Vater der Lie-be . . .

That day I moved away quickly back into the house before the passage ended. I wanted to shut out all impression of her illness—the stooped back, the brace, the cane—so that my mind, for a moment at least, might be filled with the resonance of the voice and its awesome, rhapsodic praise.

I heard someone at the front door and immediately sensed—from the exact, familiar number of nervous taps at the screen—that it was Dr. Beecroft. I went through the living room and let him in. I smelled an odor like iodine from the sagging seersucker suit even before the porch light beamed down on the bald head, the sweating brow, thick spectacles framing worried eyes that, catching sight of me, quickly tried to feign a blink of nonchalance. Some metal things in his black bag made clinks; my mind visualized crooked forceps, scissors, lances, instruments of bloodletting. "Hello, son," came the amiable voice, "up this hour?" I didn't answer, could not answer, for just as the doctor entered the hallway there was a commotion in my mother's bedroom above. We heard the noise of shuffling feet, a thumping, raised voices. The doctor hurried through the living room and up the stairs while I followed, aware that the sound, or sounds, my mother was making was no longer a scream but a choked ebb and flow of breath, as if screaming had been so bottled up by exhaustion that all that could emanate from the core of her torment was a reedy and strengthless wail. Yet somehow she managed to form words, and the words I heard were: "Jeff, Jeff! Hold me!" And when we reached the top of the stairs I was able to gaze into the room and see that my father was lifting her into his arms. *They used to argue so and bitch at each other,* I thought. *They never much touched each other in a loving way.* Florence and Miss Slocum stood by silently, watching. My father raised up the frail frame and enfolded it against his breast. His head, inclined forward, and the back of his soaked shirt prevented me from seeing my mother's face from the door where I halted, quivering; the electric fan's spindly vibration drowned out his whispers. I thought: so much arguing. Not howling and fighting like the Rowes and the Hales. But arguing, more or less politely.

I've withheld saying this for a long time, Addy, but let me say it now, I think you're a damnable snob.

Don't raise your voice like that in front of Paul—

Paul, son, kindly go outside. No, let me continue. You call Harry Bladen a drunk and you don't like his manners, and I would be the first to concede that he has perhaps too ready a penchant for the bottle. But he is one of the few enlightened co-workers I have in that mausoleum where I earn our daily bread whom I can talk to on a reasonable level of intelligence, one of the few people indeed in this entire community—yourself excluded, of course—who may have read anything but a technical book, cared for any painting above the level of Norman

Rockwell, who indeed on his own initiative has studied some formal philosophy, as I have done. If he is slightly ill-mannered around you, as you think he is—though I believe this is a figment of your imagination—it may be that he senses in you the dyed-in-the-wool reactionary you are, unable after all these years to escape your breeding among those money-obsessed, almighty-dollar-oriented northern cormorants who are your family and their friends. Your Paleozoic brother-in-law, for example, who—

Stop that! Don't talk about my family! I will not be castigated or sneered at by you or Harry Bladen or anyone else for so foolish a reason as that I expressed my distaste for Democratic politics and the works of Franklin D. Roosevelt. Millions of other people share my views. But if you and I were simply divided over politics, there would be no problem. It's this whole community, these dull-as-dishwater people, who couldn't be nicer, couldn't be more bighearted, you understand, but whom I have nothing in common with whatsoever. They've helped drive the wedge between us. For years I've tried to understand southerners, to get along with them, but I've been finally defeated by a kind of provinciality and cultural blindness unequaled anywhere in the world. Isn't it H. L. Mencken, whom you so idolize, who calls the South, correctly, the Sahara of the Bozart? If I didn't have my music I'd go insane! You can't imagine the number of times I've wished I'd never left the North, gone to New York—

You had your chance, my dear. You came very close to marrying that swank fellow from Pittsburgh, right from your neck of the woods. Why didn't you go ahead? He would have taken you out of this cultural desert.

He just might have! If I'd married Charlie Winslow I'm certain we'd have traveled somewhere at least occasionally. I'm sure he would have taken me to Paris, and I would have seen Vienna again. I might have even had one Chanel gown—nothing really extravagant, you understand, just something that a woman might like to wear once in her lifetime. Would this be asking—

Then I'm sorry you settled for so little, Adelaide. I never promised you riches. You knew that wasn't my style. The compact we made was for a home and love and companionship. I would be incapable of lavishing luxury on you, or myself, even if I cared to accumulate the money to make it possible. I've always admired much in you. But I can't admire your inability to understand that my own passions are not of tangible objects, but, if you'll pardon my saying so, of the spirit and intellect. That is why my leisure time is as valuable to me as your music is to you, and why I spend so much time in my cubbyhole upstairs writing and reading and thinking instead of scheming of ways to make money, as so many people I know do in the midst of this terrifying Depression. That is why I am and doubtless always will be a humble drone earning humble wages in a job I don't much care for. I've accepted this as a probably unalterable fact of my existence. I wish you accepted it too. I can't admire you for despising me for it—

Jeff, I don't despise—
Good night, Addy.

"I insist, Tom!" my father was saying to Dr. Beecroft. Papa had a lean, austere face with a prominent nose and wistful, reflective eyes. Now the face, usually so impassive, was blotched with distress. "You must give her more morphine! I simply insist! That pain is more than anyone can take. It's diabolical!"

"Jeff, I just don't think I can give her any more," the doctor replied. They were all in the hallway now— except for Miss Slocum—out of my mother's hearing, and I had shrunk back into the shadows near my own room, where I listened to the forbearant, expository voice. "As I told you this afternoon, people often develop a kind of tolerance, they become sensitized after long dosage. And this is what's happened to Adelaide. She's beginning to fail to absorb the injections. And also I'm simply having difficulty finding a place where the injections themselves don't cause pain. She's become so desiccated in places, you see." He paused. "What I *will* try to do is give her something else—cocaine orally, if she can possibly swallow it and keep it down. It's sometimes fairly effective. I can also try some intramuscular . . ." He went on a bit more, blah blah blah, unintelligible.

"Please do anything, Tom. There must be some way to blank out that—" He saw me at the instant I saw him. "Paul—" he said. Papa was not the calmest of men, philosophically inclined though he was. Fortunately his life had been free of *too* many disturbances. He had little natural aplomb, and even minor crises tended to get him rattled, unstrung. His thin face possessed a delicate, professorial quality more suited to reflection than to confrontation; when really agitated he got hot-eyed and, to me, a bit scary, and at the moment I felt that I had never seen him so haggard-looking, so disheveled to the forlorn depths of his spirit. "Paul, son," he said as gently as he could, "you should be in bed."

"I might as well stay up, Papa," I said. "It's almost two. I've got to carry papers at five."

"You don't have to carry papers this morning."

"Papa . . ." I hesitated, not knowing how to reply. *Why, Papa? Why not this morning, Papa? Why? Why not?*

"Listen, Paul, son . . ." He hesitated too, for the briefest instant, until Florence came to the rescue.

"Mr. Jeff," she said, "why don't you let dat boy carry his papers dis mornin'? Dey be expectin' him up at de sto'." It was her way of uttering a nontruth that cried out to be said, at least at that instant in the hallway with its mood of desperate irresolution, and I knew it was meant for me. *Everything gone be all right, baby.* "Mr. Quigley, he fire dat boy if you don't let him go."

"Then okay, son," Papa said in a parched voice, "but I still want you to try to get some sleep."

• • •

There was a kid my age named Bruce Watkins, also one of Mr. Quigley's half-dozen paper-route workers, who woke me every Sunday at dawn by throwing a handful of pebbles up at my window screen. That morning I was aroused from a murky half-sleep by the pattering noise, like a burst of sudden rainfall, which sent me upright in bed with a sensation of waking exhausted in a foreign place. I waited for the sound—the unspeakable—but heard nothing. After I put on my shorts and sport shirt and started on my way downstairs, I saw that Miss Slocum, mouth ajar, snoring faintly, was dozing at my mother's bedside. The doctor had gone. The door to my father's bedroom was closed, and this meant that he was asleep for a few minutes or perhaps merely trying to sleep in the stupefying heat, which had, even at that hour, an unnatural, almost man-made intensity, like that of the boiler room of a naval ship into which I had once been allowed to descend. Outside on the lawn the heat lay as if imprisoned in a vast scoop, breezeless, unrelieved by the disappearing night, so that the grass, which should have been drenched with dew, remained dry and brittle beneath my sneakers, and the sycamores had a drooping, withered look as the first light silvered their leaves. It was the kind of southern morning when people, waking, stirred and whispered, "Oh, Jesus." The air was sticky and ominous, the heat of the new day coming on like a cataclysm. I felt dizzy from the lack of sleep; already sweat streamed down my back. Bruce and I met at the curb and walked along the sleeping village streets toward the store. For a moment we said nothing. He was from one of those neighbor families of a cheerfully unkempt multitude I so envied. He was taller than I by six inches, older by a year, and I coveted, too, the sprinkling of facial fuzz, the occasional androgynous dip of his voice from soprano into croak, even the rosy patch of acne around his nose. He was becoming a man; I still felt in the green grip of childhood.

"How's your mama?" said Bruce finally. I sensed in his manner uncertainty, sympathy, and obligation all at once. I felt that he didn't want to talk about it any more than I did; but he knew, as I knew, that there was no way to avoid it.

"She's real sick, I guess," I replied, and then after a pause: "I mean, it's real bad."

"I sure am sorry," he said, and that was that: we both realized the subject was closed. And we leaped to the most obvious subject at hand.

"How much did you take home Friday?" Bruce asked.

"Dollar fifteen. How about you?"

"Dollar thirty. Cheap bastard. You know what Wilson told me yesterday? He told me a real interesting thing."

"What's that?" I said.

"Well, he said that he's been lifting things off Quigley for two weeks."

"Lifting things?" I said. "What kind of things?"

"Oh, you know," said Bruce, "all kinds of things. Gum. Candy. Packs of Old Golds. He gives the cigarettes to his brother. Also magazines. And a couple of those Zippo lighters on the front counter. And he lifted one of those red pillows with the picture of Roosevelt on it. He's just fed up with Quigley."

"You mean he stole them?" I said, honestly surprised. "Jesus, I wouldn't steal anything, would you?"

"Naw, not me." He paused. "Well, I took a Milky Way once last spring. More than one, really." Another pause. "Five or six."

"I guess that's not too wrong," I said, a touch enviously, then went on: "I'd quit this job, except I really need the money. Papa can't give me much in the way of an allowance. We're really getting pushed. He's got to take care of my grandmother down in North Carolina, and a bunch of the rest of the family. And this nurse Miss Slocum must cost him a fortune."

"I'd quit too," said Bruce, "maybe I'm *gonna* quit, I don't know."

Dawn bathed the village in hot, golden light. From the houses—each edged with a flower bed, each placed close to its neighbor on a trim plot of grass—came the collective drone of electric fans; a warm wind gusted out of second-story bedrooms until the dawn was filled with a somnolent hum, one hum merging with the next hum as we passed from house to house. The dogs sleeping on screened-in front porches were drugged with heat, but now and then, as we went by, a cat would uncurl itself from a stoop and cast us a squint-eyed glance, then lope away. Nearly half a century later I recall that walk with the shine of reality. There was a pleasant geometric neatness about the village with its alternating stucco and clapboard houses, linear intersecting streets, straight flagstone walks. It bore a traditional Tudor look but was too contemporary to be quaint; the ordered angularity was softened by raggedy oblongs of shade trees, hedges, shrubbery, and the whole should have been a model for the legion of bleak Levittowns and Daly Cities that were its descendants. It was the first true housing development in the nation, built by the shipyard for its white-collar workers during the Great War. The dwellings were diminutive but very well built. I insert this comment, perhaps a bit gratuitously, in order to reassure myself that the village, whatever its cramped drawbacks, was a more agreeable, far prettier place to grow up in than the mass-produced high-tech eyesores that overwhelmed the landscape in later decades. At thirteen I loved the snug neighborliness of the village, the hums of the electric fans merging together into one vast beehivelike purring as they did during that September dawn. The humming reminded me, that morning, of another marvelous continuity of sound: *Amos 'n' Andy*, the radio show that came on every weekday evening at seven o'clock. So universally adored, in the village as elsewhere, was this program and its low Negro buffoonery that on the days when I had to deliver papers late I could walk from lawn to lawn and listen to those jokes and loud guffaws booming from open windows and never miss a single beat of

the comedy line, a single nuance of the evening's episode. "De Kingfish, he is sho some dangersome *tigah*
with de wimmen!" Amos would declare, his voice a roar
from half a dozen radios. There would follow anti-
phonal roars of laughter from half a dozen shipyard
supervisors sprawled out in their tiny living rooms after
hefty evening suppers, slapping their bellies with glee
as they chewed on their Hav-A-Tampa cigars. Trudging
onward, I would not lose a word of dialogue; it cheered
me immeasurably, and lightened my toil.

I recall that morning's headline with the same clarity
that I recall any of the major wars, assassinations,
bombings, massacres, holocausts, and multiple murders
that were spread across the front pages as the century
plunged onward . . . PRAGUE AWAITS HITLER ULTIMATUM
. . . In Quigley's Store I sat on a stack of papers announc-
ing this news, and wondered when Mr. Quigley would
order us to begin stuffing our bags with the swollen
Sunday editions. They were heavy with back-to-school
advertisements, including a special forty-page insert
that celebrated the silver anniversary of Weissberger's
department store. The section's cover, I noticed, bore a
reproduction of that memorial plaque with the face of
the merchant and his, to me, perennially fascinating
nose. There had been some sort of botch with the papers
that morning; a few bundles had arrived, but there was
a shortage and as usual the blame was Ralph's. It was
his duty to meet, at four o'clock or so, the delivery truck

that came up from town, and to make sure that the proper number of bundles was unloaded; that morning Ralph had gone haywire and overlooked at least a hundred papers. Mr. Quigley was in a rage, and as I squatted there with the other boys, watching our employer emerge, Quasimodo-like, from the back room, I was thankful that his rage in its extremest form had taken place out of earshot—offstage, so to speak—since I had heard Mr. Quigley berate Ralph before for his clumsiness or his many inabilities, and it had always been a sorry performance, one that had made me want to crawl out of sight. Now Ralph emerged from the storage room, trundling after Mr. Quigley, whispering and wringing his hands, near tears; his caramel-colored moon face wore the look of transfigured animal misery that appears on the faces of severely limited people when they are the targets of fury. "Oh, boss," he pleaded in his infantile voice, "please don' fire me, please don' do dat. Momma she jes die if you fire ol' Ralph!"

"God made warthogs brighter than that burrhead," Mr. Quigley said, to no one in particular. I knew that Mr. Quigley wouldn't fire Ralph, whose services were too cheaply bought. Besides, he loved Ralph in his mindless way.

Mrs. Quigley appeared then, slapslapping in her slippers and robe from the master quarters upstairs, the cork-tipped Raleigh dangling from her lips while she already clutched a Coca-Cola. She was truly glamourless and without joy on a Sunday morning. Her slab of a face, white as veal and as yet unadorned by any of her thickly applied cosmetics, gave her the look of a Hungarian hussar officer I had seen in the movies—a cavalryman in hair curlers. "What's the matter, Quigley?" she inquired. (I suddenly recall why I never knew anything but his patronymic: no one used his first name, not even his wife.) "There is sure some goddamned commotion going on down here."

"The Nubian wonder there let them fools short us five bundles," he replied, lighting up his own cigarette and beginning to fuss with the pay phone, into which he dropped a nickel. "The genius single-handed fouls up one of the most efficient news delivery services in Virginia. Meanwhile the world teeters on the brink of catastrophe. Mankind waits to hear of its fate." It was an awful kind of show-off humor meant for us kids, his voice parroting the informed tone of Lowell Thomas, America's leading radio commentator, who, along with the newspaper headlines, was his sole source of any knowledge of current events. (He employed this style more solemnly with his customers, the afternoon idlers, who knew no better and considered him an oracle.) I clenched my teeth and closed my eyes as he continued, angrily rattling the receiver hook to signal the operator. "The Huns massing at the Czechoslovak borders, Fascism running rampant in a devastated Spain. A worsening economic crisis domestically, in spite of all forecasts. Meanwhile, at Quigley's Store there is this Nubian genius who has single-handed prevented one hundred customers from getting the news." I shut out the words, dimly heard him reach the newspaper office and howl his complaint. It all melted away into some far recess of my consciousness. I gazed straight into a display case, a glass vault of knickknacks that always disheartened me with its uninterrupted disorder, where a tribe of bottom-rung traveling salesmen had laid down a kitchen midden of small objects that never seemed to be sold and were rarely even glanced at: combs, china ashtrays, Confederate flags on gilt wooden sticks, fake leather wallets, plaster figures of Mr. Peanut, Betty Boop dolls, charm bracelets, rubber hot dogs, round boxes of sneeze powder, synthetic dog turds whose realistic sheen had, like the gloss on all the other unsellable artifacts—even those knocked down from a quarter to a dime, and to a final nickel—been dulled to a defunct grayness under a sifting of Quigleyan dust. With conscious effort I forced this gray jumble to distract me. I began to count the dolls, the combs, the ashtrays, one by one, formalizing the moment, freeing myself from my mother's image. If I woke up in hell, I thought, I'd wake up inside that junk collection.

Bruce and I set out with the available papers in our bags. The sun had risen. We flinched. After our first steps we were panting and swatting at the sweat flies that had collected under the trees—"just waiting for us," Bruce muttered. Only the birds, brainlessly cheering and chattering in the sycamores, ignored the heat. Bruce left me for his own route. On Sundays both the size and the extra number of papers required that we be replenished at various sidewalk depots spotted at intersections throughout the village. To supply these depots Mr. Quigley had bought himself, at a police auction, a used Harley-Davidson motorcycle with sidecar, which helped him fulfill some vertiginous daydream already augmented by the aviator's cap he wore, complete with earflaps, like Lindbergh's, and the Army air force officer's flight jacket he donned in all but the hottest weather. (Save for beer, the county was dry, and we all knew that he also used the gondola of the motorcycle to transport bootleg liquor, his most lucrative sideline.) The Sunday depot arrangement, unlike our weekday routine, caused us paper carriers to be absurdly prompt, since although the village was the most crime-free habitat imaginable (it would have been an insult to one's neighbors to have locked one's doors), Mr. Quigley anticipated thievery and therefore never left any of his depots alone. He impatiently mounted guard over the pile—in his seedy paramilitary outfit looking ready to shoot to kill—until one of us arrived, usually on the run, to fill up his bag again. If we were late by more than a certain number of minutes—changeable, as I recall, and set arbitrarily at his whim—we would be docked a nickel or a dime. Such a man could have escaped being murdered only during a period of economic collapse. The passage of the years has allowed me to regard Mr. Quigley with forbearance impossible for me at that time, when, not having read Dickens or Dostoevski or even an elementary work of abnormal psychology, I was unable to recognize him as one of those pitiable petty autarchs who habitually lord it over children and helpless underlings. One to despise, no doubt, but not to hate. That he was probably more than a little balmy has also occurred to me, and it should exonerate him to some degree, maybe. But I was thirteen, and lacerated. That morning all I really wanted to do was to see him dead. I was roasting. Puffing my way with my empty bag toward a rendezvous, I saw him waiting for me, his foot propped up on my pile of newspapers, glaring ominously at his watch. One of the dogs I knew along the route, an old rheumy-eyed beagle bitch I sometimes stopped to scratch, had bestirred herself and padded along after me, chops dripping. I knew I was going to be docked a nickel, perhaps a dime. It was a dime.

"I'm quitting," I said. I was astonished. The words had erupted as spontaneously as an ouch of pain.

"What did you say?"

"I'm quitting," I repeated.

"What do you mean, you're quitting?" he said. "When?"

"Right this minute," I replied. Outrage had begun to pound at my temples, and I was fast losing a coherent tongue. "Right this minute. You docked me ten cents on a day like this when it's so hot I can't even barely walk—I'm quitting right now!" My voice rose. I was still astonished. It flashed through my mind: Jesus, this is *me*, talking back. "I don't need your money, you hear?" I began to walk away past the idling motorcycle, remembering my father's scornful description of Mr. Quigley, whom he had encountered once or twice, with an effect of extreme distaste. "You damned little homunculus," I said.

"Hey, come back here, Whitehurst!" he commanded. I turned halfway about and returned his glowering gaze. "You call me a queer?" he said.

"I'm calling you a cheat and a bully," I retorted. "Leave me alone!" I turned again, began to march away.

"Now, Whitehurst, dammit, listen, come back here!" A conciliatory tone had entered his voice, along with a hint of the frantic, since I was not only leaving him in the lurch with several dozen undeliverable newspapers but engaging in a rebellion that must have been the first he had experienced. I don't think he had ever had a defector. It was bad for the image of an entrepreneur, I reflected much later, and no doubt it prompted the turnabout, sudden as lightning, that caused him to hustle after me and grab me by the arm, muttering with urgency: "Listen, I take it all back. It was just a joke, Whitehurst. I ain't gonna dock you a penny. You just take them papers and get on your route, you hear? When you finish up and come back to the store, me and you will just sit down and have us a little chat, man to man. About your debts and all. I'm a reasonable fellow. We'll share a Co-Cola or two. I should have made allowance for the heat and all, and so I take it all back, you hear?"

I capitulated as if in a trance. I said nothing, turning to the stack of papers, which I crammed painstakingly into my bag, hoisted the load to my shoulder, and walked past Mr. Quigley toward a row of stoops and front porches commencing to catch the morning's fierce, baked luminescence. The beagle tagged along for a few steps, then trotted home.

His dangerous introversion? Addy, dear, what you are now saying is preposterous. How can anything like that be a danger? And you find a little note like that written in his own handwriting and left on his bedroom table. You find that dangerous, too?

Yes, frankly, I do, for a twelve-year-old boy.

And would you mind telling me again precisely what was written in that note?

He'd left it there and gone out. I'd gone in with Florence to clean up and then I saw it. It said, as I started to tell you, "I want to——" and then the verb, beginning with f and ending with k—"I want to blank Lilly Fletcher." That's all.

You still can't say the word. At your age.

No, I can't.

Who's Lilly Fletcher?

She's one of his classmates.

Is she pretty?

Jefferson! What difference does that make? My question is, why should the boy write a note like that, and secondly, why should he leave it exposed on a table for you or me or anyone else to see it?

Maybe he found it sexually exciting to write such a note, an expression of his sexual self.

Sexual self? He's just turned twelve, for heaven's sake!

Dr. Freud, from your favorite city, says we have sexual selves when we are a few weeks old—

Don't be facetious, Jeff. Aside from that, why should he leave the note exposed—no, perhaps displayed—in such a manner?

Who knows? Maybe he just forgot all about it. Maybe he thought it might excite you or me, if we happened on it. Or Lilly Fletcher.

You're being outrageous, Jeff! That's abominable!

And you're being as usual boringly puritanical! So what if he might have found that word, and writing it in conjunction with Lilly Fletcher's name, sexually arousing? It is pronounced, incidentally, "fuck," and I should have liked many times, in the old days, to have spoken it to you, saying "fuck me fuck me," and hearing you joyfully say the same! But I couldn't ever—

Jeff! Don't!

If ever—

Don't. Don't, Jeff. I can't help what's—

I'm sorry, Addy.

Please don't bring that up again. It hurts. Don't say "old days."

I'm sorry, Addy dear. Forgive me. That was rotten of me—

I suppose I still honor the restraints in language, an old-fashioned quirk on my part.

No, I guess that it's just that I've never been able to square the relish you have for certain modern writers— James T. Farrell, for example, and Hemingway—with this, if you'll pardon me, dear, unmistakable primness.

We were talking about the boy, Jeff.

Yes?

It's not just the sex thing. It's this retreat into solitariness, this introversion I was speaking about. He's so alone most of the time, chooses to be. Not that it doesn't please me that he reads so much, adores books the way he does. And I know he loves football, at least to watch it. I don't think he's unmanly. But I'm worried about how he crawls into this shell of his, the hours and hours of solitariness. I dread the idea of him losing touch with reality—

It could be that reality's from time to time more than he can bear. Why not? It is for me.

What do you mean—what reality?

I can't say. I've been rereading Kant. Maybe when I'm finished this time I'll be able to let you know.

I love you, Jeff. I love our boy. I love him so.

Forgive me for raising my voice, Addy.

––––––––––

I walked past the houses along the route, gazing directly down the sidewalks, never pausing to deposit a newspaper at a door. The village was stirring, the early risers clumping about downstairs. Toilets flushed, here and there I heard the gurgle of a bathtub; a whiff of coffee and warm bread made my stomach churn. I plodded on. The shoulder strap of the bag, unrelieved by any lightening of the load, cut into my flesh but I barely felt the abrasion. In my craving to get where I was going, the dead weight of all that newsprint, feeling on other Sundays like pig iron, had a curious weightlessness, as if the insolent burden itself were helping to hurry me along. At the Episcopal church the sexton, an old Negro man in overalls, hosing a spray of water over a bright patchwork of dahlias and daisies, threw up a pink palm in greeting, then rolled his eyes with slow perplexity when this Sunday I failed to wave back. The river appeared, gray-blue, sparkling, an immense estuary so wide that its far shore was a thin horizontal ribbon, a hairline of dim greenery trembling like a mirage in the humid distance. I toiled onward toward the beach, crossing a strip of spongy marshland that soaked my sneakers. Then I struggled up a sandy slope, finally gained the pier. The pier! My second summer home, my hangout, my club, my Riviera, my salvation. It stretched out on barnacled timber pilings a hundred yards, terminating in a platform from which we swam at low tide or, at high tide, dove like pelicans, plunging into turbid water that all summer long was as warm as the mouth of the Amazon. It was like a Saturday night bath, and a little less clean, situated as it was only a few miles upstream from the vast shipyard and its effluvium, supplemented by other vagrant effluvia of town and village and adrift with curious doodads; an elongated, transparent fish that floated several inches from my nose was, I realized sickishly much later, a condom lazing its way toward Richmond, its purpose spent. The health worries of the period ceased at the waterside; everyone swam in the dirty James and so did I. The sun caused me to emerge from my bedroom's lonely cocoon, and that summer I had passed most every day at the pier, immersed in the brackish broth or sprawled flat on the boards in my white Lastex trunks, squinting my way through volume three of Freeman's *R. E. Lee.*

This Sunday morning the pier was almost deserted. Two Negro kids about my age were fishing for hard-shell crabs at the landing set midway out. They were not allowed to swim from the platform but could fish to their hearts' content. They were crouched immobile above their dangling strings; the stink of the gamey chicken necks they used for bait rose up like a wall of rank vapor through which I hastened, holding my breath. And the end of the pier at last. Occasionally the memories of my boyhood are framed not as if through the boy's eyes but as reflected in the viewfinder of a movie camera, drawn back on one of those marvelously unimpeded mechanisms, a boom or crane, which allows the object—in this case myself, unshouldering that iniquitous bag—to be seen as if six feet away, angling downward from about the height of a towering basket-ball player. The eye encompasses more this way: not just the newspapers, weighing two and a half pounds each, being heaved one by one into the river, but the boy shaking with rage and exhaustion, the skinny, sun-burned legs moving furiously about, sinews of the thin neck straining as, one after another, the papers are seized from the bag, heaved, drowned. A Sunday edition floats for a moment. I recall how each of the papers seemed to drift at first with a kind of lordly self-confi-dence, but then immediately afterward blotted up the water, turned from white to deathly gray, and sank out of sight, unfolding layers of itself like some diseased vegetable sea-growth. I was tempted to dive in after them to quench the heat raging around me and to assuage or at least distract myself from the returning sense of doom; but there was something too dreadful about swimming in the midst of those disintegrating fronds of paper, groping me, those headlines, bright comic pages decomposing. So I went halfway down the pier, near where the two Negro boys were crabbing, took off my clothes, and let myself slide in for a brief dip. Then as the sun rose higher I made my way back up through the village toward home.

"It's an early hour, Dr. Taliaferro," I heard Papa saying through the living-room window, "an early hour. You shouldn't have done it. It's a fruitless mis-sion."

"Jeff, I hope you don't mean that," came Dr. Talia-ferro's voice. "I'm not here to offer you anything but my presence. I want to help in any way I can."

"I'll tell you what you can do to help. Get yourself a glass from the sideboard while I try to get the ice . . . out of . . . this ice tray . . . without . . . cutting my hand off! Then you can join me while I have another belt of Old Crow."

"Something lighter, Jeff? If you'll just tell me where it is."

"In the kitchen. In the refrigerator. Ask Florence. I think she's back there. She'll find you a ginger ale or something." There was a brief silence. "Delphine, how about some *tay*. Some cool iced *tay*. 'S what they say in England. Spot of *tay*, love?"

A woman responded in a murmur, so soft that I lost the words. I could tell that Papa was a little drunk, and I felt a fresh uneasiness. He so rarely drank but when he did—Jesus, watch out. He really couldn't handle whiskey with grace, which may be why he drank so seldom; I knew there were no moral or religious scruples that kept him away from the bottle. Perhaps he was simply aware that a mere taste of alcohol turned him garrulous and indiscreet, made his humor heavy-handed, unlimbered his tongue in a most aggressive way, causing him also to speak in a high, penetrating tone as he was doing now. He was addressing Dr. Harri-son Taliaferro, pastor of the First Presbyterian Church. The name was pronounced Tolliver, one of those antique Virginia mutations that had amused my mother (along with the Sclater that became Slaughter, St. John turned into Sinjin, Montague losing its terminal vowels to rhyme with Sontag) nearly as much as the minister's creamy baritone and aging-matinee-idol pulpit manner had amused me. He had cracked us up—we pubescent apes who sat in the back pew bursting with imprisoned giggles, flaring our nostrils, clenching our jaws, turning our palms outward in pious entreaty in unison with his own, listening to not a word of those ardent marathon sermons preached from beneath the arched gospel legend in gold leaf: BE YE DOERS OF THE WORD NOT HEARERS ONLY. To my knowledge he had never visited our house, but here he was, Nelson Eddy himself. I could see him through the window, seated together with his broad-bosomed wife—motherly, twisting a big flowered handbag—who was staring directly at my father. She wore a damp, puckered look tinged with alarm. Seconds before there must have been sorrow, now there was disapproval. Shock.

"No tay then?" my father went on. "May I continue in my endeavor to explain why I am a hypocrite?"

"Jeff, please," protested the minister, "this is a terrible time for you. I don't want you to feel it necessary to unburden yourself—"

"I'm not unburdening myself, Dr. Taliaferro," he interrupted. "Since when was the truth a burden to an honest man? And I trust I can call myself honest. I'm deficient enough in most other virtues. But I'll tell you,

Doctor, it's neither easy nor much fun to be a good hypocrite, especially if one is honest. Your run-of-the-mill dishonest hypocrite—and I'd say that the breed composes a substantial majority of your congregation—doesn't really object to all the fraudulent trappings of religion, the vain ceremonials, the ceremonial vanities, the bland absurdities of this ritual called worship. Metaphorically speaking, he devours these sanctimonious goodies because they taste good not to his soul but to his ego. They thrill that most sensitive part of his palate, which is his self-esteem. In his core he knows how empty, how false all this obscene obsequiousness is, but, you see, he is a dishonest hypocrite and therefore it causes him no pain. On the other hand, I, being an *honest* hypocrite—that is not an oxymoron, Doctor—have throughout the decade or so of my service to your business—pardon me, to your house of worship—felt extreme distress. This is whether it be sitting on a Sunday absorbing your incomparable wisdom, or teaching a Sunday school class, as I have so many times, the absolutely riveting fact that in Deuteronomy it is written that thou shalt not plow with an ox and an ass together—and have given in my heart a private twist to those words 'plow' and 'ass'—or at a Wednesday night meeting of the deacons, when for two hours my bones have ached with ennui and my brain with Christian banality. I have felt pain. I have felt—forgive me the comparison—crucifixion."

There was a pause. "I hate your abominable religion!" He halted again, then resumed more gently: "You both have been nothing but decent to me. I wish I'd gotten to know you better. But now I'd appreciate it if you all would leave this house. Do refresh yourself with a drink, though, beforehand. We can talk about other matters. I know you're a baseball fan, Doctor. Who's got the National League pennant this year?"

The silence was complete. The minister and his wife were not only struck dumb but made stiff, remaining motionless where they sat. While Papa had spoken, I had lingered at the edge of the lawn, at curbside, next to the sheriff's QUIET ZONE sign that had been put up a couple of weeks before. Now when Papa fell silent I moved away from the sign, out of the cool octagon of its shade, and walked across the lawn to the house. Yet I dared not yet go in. I hung back on the small front porch, watching the trio in the living room. Glimpsed in the morning shadows, they were like effigies: Papa, in his shirtsleeves, leaning against the mantelpiece with a drink in his hand, frowning down at the floor; on the sofa Dr. Taliaferro, looking as if he had seen the devil, a werewolf, a rabid bat; his wife seated next to him, her eyes seeking immediate rescue, holding an indrawn breath while her lips described an almost perfect round voiceless "O!"

Finally the minister spoke with a curious wheeze, without strength. "You've been a steadfast and dedicated man, Jeff. How can you say all this? Why?"

"Because I *execrate* God, if he exists."

There was an aspirated hiss of air from Mrs. Taliaferro. I heard her whisper: "Oh, please, God."

"Jeff!" exclaimed Dr. Taliaferro. "Oh, Jeff!"

"Please, God," his wife whispered again.

"Nor do I have faith in his only begotten son, our Lord and Savior, Jesus Christ."

"Oh, no," came the wife's whisper again.

"Jeff. Jeff. Jeff." I saw the minister tremble.

After a moment Papa spoke slowly. "An hour or so ago when that jewel whom you met, Miss Slocum, awoke me to tell me that Adelaide had fallen into a coma, I felt the greatest relief I've ever known. For several years there hasn't been a day when she hasn't felt pain. For the past few weeks that pain has been excruciating, despite the analgesics that modern medicine has designed to quell suffering like hers. And for the last few days that pain . . ." He halted, passed his fingers over his brow, went on: "What can I say? I never knew it was possible for a human being to endure such torture. There hasn't been an hour during this past weekend when I haven't longed to have a gun so I could put her out of all that."

"Oh, God," I heard Mrs. Taliaferro breathe.

"If the Lord giveth, which I heard you say at a funeral not too long ago, and if the Lord taketh away, which I also heard you proclaim with such sturdy acceptance, is not the Lord accountable for what happens in the time between the giving and the taking? Is he not, I ask you, accountable for Addy's monstrous suffering? *Cursed* be the name of the Lord!"

"Please!" I heard Mrs. Taliaferro's small, wild wail. "No more!" She was recoiling from my father now, recoiling back against the pillows of the chair as if from a reptile. "I can't bear this!"

Dr. Taliaferro rose, put forth a hand. "Jeff, you're distraught! Please try not to say any more right now! For the love of God, no more blasphemy!"

Miserable, I wanted to stop my father—not for what he was saying but for fear he might become unpinned and fly out into space. But I didn't know what to do. I couldn't interrupt, yet neither could I stay to hear more. I was suddenly washed over by shivery fatigue, and I still felt a sandy clamminess from my swim. I longed to go upstairs and fall into bed, but for some reason I shrank from making my presence known in the midst of this hysteric ruckus. So I decided to walk somewhere until the Taliaferros left, and had already made a move to sneak away from the porch when my father's voice— overlaid by a vaguely ominous accent I had seldom heard except when alcohol unlatched the closet where he stored his demons—jolted me, arrested me in mid-step, turned me like a top. For an instant I thought he had begun to clutch the lapels of Dr. Taliaferro's beige Palm Beach suit. But my eyes were tricked. He had drawn so close to the minister, though—face to face— that I felt that they were surely exchanging breaths, and I saw a trickle from my father's drink slide slowly down his wrist, leaking drop by drop onto the immaculate beige sleeve. I thought: That preacher looks like he's going to pass out.

"Dr. Taliaferro, are you acquainted with Arthur Schopenhauer?" Papa said.

"Yes—yes," the minister stammered, "I believe so. An atheistic philosopher. I heard about him when I was studying at the seminary, years ago."

"Lucretius? Voltaire? Montaigne? Bertrand Russell? Nietzsche?"

"Yes. All atheists. Especially that last fellow."

"I only want to say this, Doctor, before I ask you once again to leave. I want to say that during the eight or ten years that I've served as one of your deacons I've spent countless hours upstairs in the little cubicle I call my study reading the words of these men. I'm a poorly educated person, trained for engineering, but I've wrestled with these thinkers, trying to puzzle out their understanding of human existence. I've learned to read a little French, and German fairly well, that's how much some of these men have meant to me. Not a one of them really offers much hope for mankind; they see the course of human destiny as an inexplicable one full of strife and suffering. Or filled with random vicious energies utilized mainly to stave off boredom. A wretched view. But this is the truth as they've seen it. Ha!"

Papa faltered for a moment, took a sip of his drink, and then, still glaring at the minister, said: "Meanwhile

your deacon here with the twinkly eyes has been helping to officiate at Holy Communion, passing up the
aisles with little lozenges of Wonder bread and thimble-
fuls of Welch's grape juice in the service of the Lord's
Supper, although if truth really be known, my only
anticipated pleasure, really, was to eye the bare knees of
a few of the prettiest members of the congregation. You
have no idea, Dr. Taliaferro, how carelessly provocative
have been the possessors of some of those knees. Absolutely true, Delphine." He cast a glance at Mrs. Taliaferro, whose face was as bloodless as a peeled potato,
rigid, and rather wild-eyed. "But when not up to such
skullduggery," he went on, "I have been tormented by
perpetual doubt. I have so often questioned my own
integrity, wondering how a man of my skepticism could
serve an institution and subscribe to a belief that offers
such false promises of bliss, here now and in the here-
after. Now I have no more doubt about my doubt. In the
incomprehensibility of my wife's agony I have found a
terrible answer of sorts. If there is a God, he cares
nothing for humankind. I will not believe in such a
God! If such a God exists, then I abominate him! Please
go away now. I must go upstairs and be with Addy."

"Jeff, oh, Jeff," the minister exclaimed, "you're not
the first Christian to doubt God's wisdom and the inscrutable mystery of his ways in the face of bitter grief.
But always there is this wondrous return to faith——"

"Enough!" my father cried. "Enough! Please get the
hell out of here! Vain and silly quack anyway!" The

glass fell from between his fingers and soundlessly collided with the carpet, missing by a hair one of Dr. Taliaferro's brown-and-white wing-tip shoes. "Nietzsche said it in a word about men like you. You make me want to wash my hands!"

I fled. I fled running at top speed. Anything to get away from that discord. I ran in a seizure of fright, wanting to escape from the little house that I loved, shrouded with its dark calamity. I ran down a sycamore-shaded street, listening to the *pop-pop* of my sneakers against the sidewalk, running in the windless heat until the heat itself, thick as fur, slowed me down to a listless walk. The village was coming awake. Those sentinel radios had begun to blare from the open windows. I heard hallelujahs as some evangelist got down to work. The air was starting to bloom with the Sabbath's twitter and cacophony—Sunday school choruses, pipe organs, Baptist hymns, the croon of preachers. I scuffed along aimlessly up one light-dappled street, then down another, a somnambulist; never had I felt so tired. As they did every Sunday, Flying Fortresses in formation from the Army airfield droned low over the village, the engines a massed mutter at first, then swelling into a racket that hurt the eardrums, deafened. For a long moment the planes darkened the sun and the sycamores quivered beneath a torrent of vibrations. I stopped and stood still, peering upward through the shadows cast by the wings, waiting for the flight to pass. In a quick hallucination, vivid and unalarming, I saw the planes transformed: a flock of Nazi bombers dumping their cargo over the village, then vanishing like birds.

I'm not teasing, Jeff. You will want to marry someone like Martha Flanders. She's a great beauty.

Not as beautiful as thee, my darling. But let's not talk about that—

She has an eye for you, I know. She has gorgeous legs. I've seen her in a bathing suit. A very naughty divorcée. I'm sure she's going to want you.

Addy, dear, let's not talk about that.

I resumed walking and saw Bruce Watkins coming down the far side of the street, a fishing pole over his shoulder. He had changed from his paper-route trousers into swim trunks and T-shirt, and his face had a look of worry.

"Hellfire, Paul!" he said. "Where you been? Old Man Quigley's about off his rocker trying to figure out where you went to."

"I don't care," I answered.

"What happened?"

"Nothing," I said. "I got tired."

"What happened to your papers?"

When I didn't reply and walked on, Bruce said: "Old Man Quigley's in a real fit. First he was mad, then he got kind of scared. He was saying, 'Think of the hell to pay, one of my employees gets kidnapped—' "

"I don't care," I said. I turned around. Something

impelled me homeward. Bruce called to me again, but I didn't hear the words. His cry trailed me through the phantasmagoria of the morning, a landscape made more strange because of my jittery exhaustion and my scratchy, unfocused eyes, which changed the known into the bizarre: a spaniel panting on a stoop into a leering zoo carnivore, flower beds into a blur of Technicolor, lawn sprinklers into grandiose fountains. Once in my near-trance I stumped my toe against the sidewalk's upthrust warp and came close to sprawling on the grass.

Then, just as I reached the house and took a step onto the lawn, I heard my mother singing. I stopped. Chill after chill coursed through me at the sound of that anthem, soaring clear and jubilant in the still air, undiminished in strength and certitude, incantatory as ever in the way it voiced its utterance of loving praise. Mother is going to live, I thought feverishly. She's risen from bed. She's singing. She's going to be well·like Florence said she'd be.

Ist auf deinem Psalter,
Vater der Lie-be . . .

Yet the moment of astonishing joy into which I had been freed was, like the voice itself, an illusion, and this I realized almost immediately, sensing the foolishness of my expectation and the mistake. For why would a chorus of men be accompanying my mother, as it was now, and an orchestra too? Hope evaporated, disappeared. I went into the house, passed through the living room and down the hallway to my mother's sanctuary, from which the music was coming, and then heard the familiar *tick-tick* of the worn record, spinning on the turntable of the phonograph. I crept into the music room, trying to make no sound. There my father stood with a hand propped against the wall, brooding on the sun-drenched lawn and the flower beds while the steel needle tracked its way across the sizzling shellac grooves and let the room fill with this final passage of Brahms, turned up to the highest volume, so that the hymnal sonorities of the music, enveloping all—the busts of Schubert and Brahms and Beethoven, the portraits of the great virtuosi, the image of my mother herself, captured in a flicker of bygone merriment—shook me again with such ferocity that for an instant I thought I could see her there, seated at the piano by the window, her voice raised exultantly as it had been long before. But then the record came to an end and Papa removed the needle.

"Paul, son," he said, "where have you been? You look so tired. You all right? Do you have a fever? You must go to sleep."

"I was staying down at the pier, Papa," I replied. "I didn't want to come home right away."

"Yesterday she wanted me to play this for her," he explained, "but I couldn't. I guess I forgot. I wanted to play it for her anyway. It's Lotte Lehmann. Her favorite singer, you know." His voice was clotted with the feeble huskiness of immense fatigue. He tottered and he raised his twitching fingers to his face, alarming me. But then he ran his fingers nervously over his lips as I had seen him do before in these seizures, a pantomime both sly and clumsy, trying to mask the odor of alcohol. He shouldn't be drinking, I thought again, even now in all of this. Dreading such moments as I did, I shrank from him not through any threat or fear of disorder but because in his new disguise, that of a stranger, he was unpredictable and unfatherly, a freak. And at that instant, as if to demonstrate the outlandish behavior that cowed me and made me want to flee him, he fell to his knees on the floor in front of me and crooked his arm around my waist, pulling me close and pressing his head against my shoulder. The impetuous, almost savage, embrace—his furious gust of emotion—took me off guard and made me give an inward groan. Kneeling, he clung to me as a drowning man would, and for long seconds he felt as if he might pull me down; but then he let go of me, and in the buoyant release I drew back and beheld his rage and pain.

"Paul, son," he blurted, too loud, "remember this morning! Remember what I have to say! Remember this morning!" And once more he grasped me tightly.

Numb with despair, I could say nothing.

"Repeat these words after me. Are you listening?

141

Although earth's foundations crumble and the mountains be shaken into the midst of the seas . . . Are you listening? Say them after me!"

"*Although earth's foundations crumble* . . ." I faltered and fell silent.

"Say them after me, son!" He gripped me hurtfully.

"Papa!" I implored him, weeping.

"*Yet alone shall I prevail!* That's what you must understand, son. *Yet alone shall I prevail!* Say it after me!"

"*Although earth's foundations crumble and the mountains be shaken* . . ."

"*Into the midst of the seas!*"

"*Into the midst of the seas!*" I echoed.

"*Yet alone shall I prevail!*"

We each devise our means of escape from the intolerable. Sometimes we can fantasize it out of existence. I recall repeating in bewilderment the words he commanded me to say—"*Yet alone shall I prevail!*"—while my mind composed such other words as would distract me from the moment's anguish. My name is Paul Whitehurst, it is the eleventh of September, 1938, when Prague Awaits Hitler Ultimatum. Thus lulled by history, I let myself be elevated slowly up and up through the room's hot, dense shadows. And there, floating abreast of the immortal musicians, I was able to gaze down impassively on the grieving father and the boy pinioned in his arms.